Michelle Steinbeck was born in Lenzburg, Switzerland in 1990. She writes prose, poetry and drama; reportage and columns. She works as editor-in-chief at *Fabrikzeitung* and is the organiser of *Babelsprech*, a forum for young international poetry. *My Father was a Man on Land and a Whale in the Water* is her first novel. It was shortlisted for the Swiss Book Prize 2016 and longlisted for the German Book Prize 2016. Steinbeck lives in Basel.

Jen Calleja is a writer and literary translator from German based in London. She has translated literary fiction and non-fiction by Wim Wenders, Gregor Hens, Kerstin Hensel and Marion Poschmann, and her translations have been featured in *The New Yorker*, *The White Review* and *Literary Hub*. In 2017/18, she was the inaugural Translator in Residence at the British Library.

MICHELLE STEINBECK

My Father was a Man on Land and a Whale in the Water

Translated by Jen Calleja

DARF PUBLISHERS,
LONDON

Published by Darf Publishers, 2018

Darf Publishers Ltd
277 West End Lane
West Hampstead
London
NW6 1QS

My Father was a Man on Land and a Whale in the Water
By Michelle Steinbeck

English Translation Copyright © Jen Calleja, 2018

First published in German by Lenos Verlag (Switzerland) in 2016 as
Mein Vater war ein Mann an Land und im Wasser ein Walfisch

*This book has been translated thanks to a grant awarded by the Swiss
Arts Council Pro Helvetia.*

Cover image by Nonda Coutsicos

Printed and bound in Great Britain by Clays Ltd, Elcograf S.p.A.

ISBN-13: 978-1-85077-318-4

For Sandra and Sophie

I want to know it all, all about me, about you, about all the people that are about to live, about the buried fiddlers, I want to speak all languages and talk to every human every night.

Katja Plut, *To Become a Human*

The Kid

There's a child in the yard, its shoes flash every time it takes a step.

It carefully places one foot in front of the other until it comes to a stop in front of me. It looks up, nose streaming, and says: Last night I dreamt that I insulted everyone.

I turn off onto the gravel path without looking back and the kid crows a barrage of abuse after me.

A bird is sitting on the washing line chirping and rolling a hempseed in its beak. The springtime sun shines straight in my face.

The door to the building is open.

My room is just as I'd left it. Rumpled bedclothes on the mattress, crooked piles of books, empty clothes hangers in the open wardrobe. It smells funny, I open the window. A draught whirls tiny feathers out of the birdcage onto the table, over the cast iron teapot and my father's typewriter. I run my finger through the dust on the keys, press, the little foot jumps up to the ribbon and back down again. I pull the typewriter to the edge of the table, my fingertips rest expectantly on the keys; I've already thought it all through on my way here.

I'm getting hot. I impatiently shake my coat from my shoulders, stand up, and hang it on the hook. What did I want to do? I wander restlessly around the room, go from the window to the door, from the door to the bed, from the bed to the table. I pick up things: a chewed pencil, a tarnished silver spoon, a crumpled pack of cigarettes, a matchbox with a picture of a half-naked roller-skating sailoress on it. I push the table over to the window, fumble a cigarette out of the pack, straighten it out and light up; the smoke goes straight in my eyes. Down in the street I see the kid with the flashing shoes. It's tugging stubbornly on a blooming gorse bush. A branch breaks off, the kid tentatively hits it against its leg, then whips the bush; the blossom sprays, the kid shrieks wildly.

The sun has crawled behind the smokestack, a crow is sitting on it cracking a nut. I feed a new sheet of paper into the typewriter and start pecking at the keys: *My father was a man on land and a whale in the water.*

I stay there until I get hungry, then I get up and go into the kitchen. The refrigerator is empty, there's only a pack of deep frozen spinach in the freezer compartment. I slam the refrigerator door shut and let out a scream. The kid with the flashing shoes is standing in the doorway.

What are you doing in my home?, I shout.

The kid stares at me wide-eyed. Then it turns on its heel and runs down the hallway into the living room; I see it bang the door behind it.

Now wait a minute!, I say. If there's one thing I despise, it's ill-behaved children.

I stand in front of the closed door, consider what devastating thing I'm going to say, then pull down the handle.

The room is filled with smoke. Swathes of it drift like shaken out bed sheets, a dozen children's heads jut up out of it. They're brooding around the living room table. The cloying stench of unwashed hair and fermented milk hangs in the air. I wrench open the window. The cloud of smoke gently peels away from the children and skims over the windowsill on its way out. Now I can see them properly, their unwholesome little figures: burnt brows, smears of ash on their cheeks, limp locks, patchy fluff on their top lip, bent backs and drooping necks. Fish eyes in pale faces run fitfully over the table, over tarnished compact mirrors, fag ends in congealed candlewax, overflowing ashtrays, burn holes; they focus on a thread of smoke rising from the pipe of the only boy sitting upright. He's enthroned in a huge leather armchair and smokes with the air of a king. He opens his eyes, purses, then smacks his lips. The little sulphur-yellow clouds rising from his jaws transform into curls. He watches them, how they distend and decay, puts his pipe down, and looks me in the face.

Are you hungry?

He's balancing my spotted breakfast bowl in one hand, the colour has already chipped off around the edge. He's shovelling muesli into his mouth with a soup spoon. He munches and laughs, white milk runs down his dumb chin. His round jug ears are pricked, and the three blonde hairs sprouting from his Adam's apple eyeball me jeeringly. He has a pretty face, just like I do.

You must be hungry, my brother says with his mouth full, you were always the family's rubbish chute.

My scalp itches, and I quickly scratch it.

Still got lice?, he sneers. Aren't you a bit old for that?

A couple of the children laugh. My heart pulses in my throat.

He holds out the bowl of muesli, runs his free hand through his hair, shrugs his shoulders and places the bowl on the table. He clicks his fingers, and from all around quick little hands appear, flitting over the table, dabbing at residual powder and particles of tobacco and nimbly rolling them in little papers. A small boy is concentrating hard on a peculiar model, his tongue sticking out between his lips; my brother takes the thing out his hands and holds it right under my nose. In a childish voice he mews: Look at the nice thing I made! An aeroplane.

Actually, it's quite refined: a cigarette fuselage with cigarette wings. My brother smirks in my face. Curses swell up and sink in my mind, I breathe in and out deeply.

Bravo, I say dryly and clap my hands, magnificent. You've really come far. But now the party's over, I'm back, I reign here!

I fall silent, I hear my voice reverberating – how ridiculous it sounds.

He snorts and smiles at me pityingly: You've never had a clue, have you. Did you bring any cash?

I throw myself at him and beat my fists against his chest. He laughs, coughing. A girl stirs half asleep at his feet. She opens her eyes and sits up arduously, my brother strokes her hair. She lays her head in his lap and in a dark voice talks of apples and a party where everyone had made themselves up so beautifully, with shawls and fine clothes, and how she simply died there.

I lock the door of my room behind me and lie down on the bed. I cross my hands behind my head, the sun shines in through the window straight into my face. The humiliation churns hotly inside me. How disgusting my brother is! And those sickly brats, what makes them think they can laugh at me?

I lie there stiffly and cook up punishments. I'll make them sausages and mashed potato and slug poison, and they'll gobble it down and writhe around on the floor whimpering. And then, when they've finally recovered and are taking their first shaky steps outside, I'll run them over with a field roller.

I roll over towards the wall and pull the covers up over my head. I close my eyes and breathe loudly into the cavity. A carousel races around behind my forehead, right beneath my eyelids. Blurred lights streak by, and beyond them miniscule flies' legs perform a Russian dance in fast forward.

A scorching flat iron presses down on my chest, I spring up and throw it out of the window. There's a dull thud. I look down below. There's the iron. And there's the kid with the flashing shoes. I look around my room for something to throw out after it. My heart is thumping.

Despicable brats. Dare to play tricks on me! I lean out of the window – the kid isn't moving. I leave my room, press my ear against the living room door. Not a sound.

The kid is lying on its stomach. The iron has dug a decent hole out the back of its head. I poke the kid with my foot and look around acting bewildered, as if I'd just come across it by chance. I pace up and down, look left and right inconspicuously, and turn the kid onto its back. I give it a slap in the face and hold its nose. Its shoes are still flashing. I shudder. Why did it have to be standing under my window of all places! I grab the kid by the wrists and haul it through the gravel.

I take the kid to my room and lean it against the wall. I close the door behind me, fall onto the bed. The kid slides onto the floor and across the parquet.

Bah, I say loudly, and rub away the goose flesh on my arms.

The kid gawps up at the ceiling, its milk teeth twinkling in its open mouth. Fluff has got caught in its curls. I touch its hand. It's cold. I hang the kid over the radiator and sit on the bed. I smoke two cigarettes, one after the other. Then I feel sick. I crossly smell my fingers and look at the kid. It's still hanging over the radiator. I close my eyes.

I can already hear them sneaking about in the hallway. Their sluggish feet drag along the floor, they whisper to one another, they can smell it through the wall. They want to bundle me up in a sheet and light my hair, inhale deeply, draw me into their small, grey organs and blow me back out until I'm nothing but ash.

I get up and leave the house. I hear a jingling and jangling; I see a hillock dotted with white sheep. An old farmer wearing a flat cap is hobbling after them. He throws himself onto the slowest one. He binds its legs together and strokes its head. I see his cracked teeth when he says: Yes, yes, I like the sheep very much, but when they're old no one wants to eat them anymore.

The sheep bucks with its bound legs. The children stand around me in a circle and stamp their flashing shoes on the ground. They chant: Feed, feed, feed us!

The sheep won't be enough, the farmer says, and blows on his whistle. A white cow strolls over, beautifully speckled with black spots. It takes a look around with its big eyes, and the farmer draws out a gun. I start to cry. I put on a variety of hats and perform a Russian dance for the farmer, but it's no use. He pulls the trigger.

I wake with a start. The kid's gone. I thump the wall, elated and relieved. I listen at the wall to the living room: nothing.

How nice not to have a kid's corpse with a runny head to worry about. The peculiar things we dream up! How long was I asleep for? I get up and see the kid's hand poking out from under the radiator. It's stuck headfirst and awkwardly twisted between the wall and the radiator, and its pale little legs with their filthy striped socks are sticking up out of the ends of its ridden up trousers. I pull the kid out, it's soft and warm and creased. Its dented face is even more vacant than it was before – disgusting, I cry out, this is disgusting. I rub my hands down my trousers. Now I feel very hungry. I feel it so severely that I can no longer move, everything has become numb all of a sudden. I stagger into the kitchen, search the cupboards and the refrigerator, and find the frozen spinach. I take the packet into my bedroom and put it on the radiator.

I suck on a clot of spinach in bed. It tastes vile. I chuck it at the kid's damaged head. Then I drag down my father's old leather suitcase from the top of the wardrobe and unsnap the clasps. I shake crumpled shirts, moth balls and yellowed books out onto the floor and heave the kid into the suitcase. I fold its legs up over its head, cross its arms over them, close the lid, sit on top of it, tuck in a couple of stubborn fingers, and click both golden clasps shut.

Back out in the street there are three crows. They hop out of my way and ogle me, their little heads tilted to one side. I swing the suitcase, they fly off.

The Soothsayer

Two unkempt children are sitting on the cemetery wall. They flick fag ends at me. I pretend not to notice and hurry past them. I push the suitcase on ahead of me as discreetly as possible.

They're always smoking, I mumble, disgusting!

The children whisper and snicker; I turn a corner and look back, they stay where they are on the wall. Though the children are the only other souls in the cemetery, I pick my way through the gravestones for a long time on the lookout for a shielded spot where I can dig a hole undisturbed.

The grave looks fresh, the earth is dark and loosely heaped – it seems like a good plot and pleasant to boot: the dead want to be among the dead. The young medical student hasn't been down there for very long, surely he feels out of place and overwhelmed by all the wreaths, stuffed animals and the candles arranged in the shape of a heart. One moment he was dissecting corpses, his fingers trembling with excitement, and now he's one himself – he must be so bored in that box! I shovel the grave free of its offerings with both hands. The kid ought to lie on top of his coffin so that they can babble each other to sleep and get used to being dead together, down in the earth.

The spleen was completely mouldy, the student will boast, that's how long it had been in formalin, I almost threw up!

And the kid will brag about its leader, my brother, who could blow smoke rings at the age of eight.

I begin to dig, I scratch into the earth with my bare hands, excavate small stones and root nodes, shovel crumbling dirt with the edges of my palms. The soil is hard like in winter. It's far off of being a hole, a hollow perhaps, barely big enough for a canary, and the dirt is already pressing in underneath my fingernails. I tug on a bedded in rose bush and cut up my fingers on the thorns. My cursing is carried away on the wind, and the little filth that I've managed to scrape up swirls over the graves like desert sand. I sit down on the suitcase and pick out the dirt from under my nails. Only now do I realise that I'm shaking, my stomach contracts with hunger. I roll a burning candle from the graveside between my fingers to warm them a little. Suddenly I'm overcome with a shudder, and wax sprays my coat. I bawl from feeling so weak, and because my hands are bleeding, and from the pressure underneath my nails. An icy drop of water splashes on my neck, I rub it away and kneel on the rock-hard earth once more. It starts to rain. The wind whips my hair into my face, and the rain fills the meagre hole with water, but I keep digging and I don't stop.

The storm clamours around me. I push the heavy suitcase between the gravestones down the gravel path; it cleaves a deep trench into it, the stream of rain runs straight into my shoes.

What have you been eating! I howl at the suitcase, emptying them out.

I search for the gate, trying to recognise anything, but the wind shakes my head as if it were an acorn ripe for knocking down from a tree. Branches crash down onto the graves, hailstones pelt my face; I hold on tightly to the suitcase and edge us onwards with small steps. The outline of an archway finally emerges in the sheet rain, I make my way over to it and take shelter beneath it.

It is strangely silent under the arch.

Its stones are ancient, eroded and overgrown with moss. Ferns and withered climbers droop from its curved roof. I shake out my hair and hope that no beetles fall on my head. It's odd: behind me the wind howls, but ahead it seems quiet and clear.

I listen, and think, and step out from the other side of the arch.

There's no storm here. The sun is dozing beneath a yellow haze, and the smooth cobblestones quietly gasp beneath my soles. The path is straight, flanked by high fir trees trimmed into cones. Between them I can see fields of stone figures with gold engravings. The tombs of the rich.

How about that, I say quietly, didn't I tell you cemeteries were nice.

The avenue leads to another archway, behind which stands a mighty construction. Roman columns, a domed roof, smoke rising from it. A shadow falls over me in front of the arch, I look up. Up on plinths are women's breasts and severe men's faces; two sphinxes, they blink. I close my eyes and pass through.

A courtyard, a fountain, a pond with small grey fish. Around it walls, columns, a cloister. At its centre a staircase leads all the way up to the four stoutest columns bearing a roof inscribed with golden lettering.

Flame, undo that which is ephemeral.
Liberated is the eternal.

I climb the steps, pause in front of the cast iron door embellished with small crosses. I knock. Nothing. I knock again. My knuckles now ache. It remains silent. I pull down the heavy door handle, the door can be pushed open, it isn't locked.

I step inside. The door closes heavily behind me. Deathly silence and gloom. Further back, however, at the end of the corridor, a weak light, a bluish shimmer. My arm held out in front of me, I grope my way towards it. The light is coming from a gap in a low, half-open iron door. I creep towards it and peep inside: an oven! Inside, an old woman sits hunched at a round table covered with red velvet. On the table are playing cards, she slowly turns one, and then another. Her face is lined with furrows and ash eyeliner. She has blue hair and is baring her teeth.

I shudder.

The old woman raises her head and stares through the crack in the door. I freeze and think: she can't possibly see me out here in the dark.

Oh, there you are, she says and waves me in. Her voice is hoarse and croaky.

I hop from one foot to the other, my heart thumps loudly. I prise open the heavy door with both hands. I duck my head and climb into the oven. I take a step towards the old woman. Then I quickly sit down on the suitcase and boldly jiggle my legs.

It's dark in here too, it's only around the old woman that an uncanny light radiates, as if she's glowing; maybe it's her hair. She wriggles around on the chair and pulls her silver dress up over her knees. Then I see movement in the darkness of her lap. Out crawls a beast, a tiny, wizened, furry crocodile. I gulp, the hairy reptilian creature opens a toxic-yellow eye and snarls, before nestling awkwardly on the old woman's legs. She splays her gout-ridden fingers in its fur and wraps her own hair around her throat like a stole. Her eyelashes are monstrous and most certainly stiff, like her breasts, which peep out of her dress.

Reading cards is my calling, the old woman says, and offers me a cigarette.

I wriggle around cheekily on the suitcase.

You take yourself very seriously you old crone, I mumble to myself and twist my wet hair between my fingers.

I'm suspicious of young people who have never smoked, the old woman says, as if she hadn't heard me. Smoking is a way of life.

I snatch the fag from her claw, and she hands me the cards. She leans forward, her blue hair sweeps over the floor, her spidery hands paw around under the little table –

Shuffle and stack the deck, she grumbles, sitting up with a groan, a wooden box in her hands.

I clamp the cigarette between my lips and fudge two piles of cards together. I was never any good at that elegant, fanning sort of shuffling; I wiggle and shove the cards, which reluctantly slide past one another, some fall on the floor. Ash from my cigarette falls on my legs. My eyes water.

The old woman observes me narrowly.

Shuffling is the most important part, she says, you mix your soul into it.

She opens the little box and draws out a small wooden pipe. She lights it and passes it to me. I inhale the sweet smoke, try to feel at one with the cards and purposefully lay down a stack with each exhale. As soon as I release the final cards from my hand, gently brushing against the velvet, the soothsayer snatches the pipe from me and greedily smokes it up.

The figures on the cards blur, I screw up my eyes and try to sharpen their outlines, it makes me light-headed. I straighten my back, and a knock comes from the suitcase – I freeze, and the knock comes again, it really does, from the inside!

Are you listening to me? The soothsayer prods the air in front of my eyes with a crooked finger.

You're not in the centre, see, she says, poking a card, you ought to be in the centre of things.

I listen. Yes, it's true, something is knocking in the suitcase, very quietly, I can feel it on my legs. I scrutinise the old woman: has she noticed anything?

You don't participate, the old woman says without changing her expression, and traces a circle over the cards with her gnarled fingers, even though this is your life.

I kick the suitcase with my heel.

There's still a lot of child in you, the old woman sighs. A long journey… The father is the problem: You are very close to the father… A separation… Fears.

The soothsayer leaves long pauses and runs her fingertips over the cards. I keep my face blank and listen out for movement inside the suitcase.

The old woman closes her eyes and struggles for breath, her chest rattling: Your fears and your hesitation are not yours… They are your father's – pack them in the suitcase and give them back to him!

I have to cough all of a sudden: What, I ask coughing, what did you say?

Open your heart, the old woman proclaims, love paves the way for you. The Knave of Hearts is beside you, and the Love Letter. Even the Wedding Bells!

I don't want them, I say. But what was that about the suitcase?

The crocodile-dog growls, and the old woman chastises me with a dark look. She has scarab-green eyes painted on her lids.

The father stands in your way. He's blocking the lucky cards. The highest Fortune card is there, and the Triumph card too! Give the father back his suitcase, and you shall be showered with love, fame and gold.

The soothsayer nods contentedly and takes a pull on the dead pipe.

I see, I say, my father. He flew the coop a long time ago – He was afraid of children. I don't know my father anymore and his suitcase belongs to me now, just like everything else he left behind.

You're dragging his suitcase around with you, the old woman says exasperatedly, its contents belong to him, not you!

She gives me a piercing look, and then suddenly her eyes begin to roll – first one, and then the other, in different directions.

A red house, the old woman says in a new, crystal clear voice, in the red city. You will find him there. You must hurry.

I don't say anything. The old woman lays down the final card.

Oh, she says, startled, and the creature in her lap stirs and begins to slobber and retch, I see fair men in your future!

I raise my eyebrows, intrigued.

It's getting worked up, the old women explains and strokes the scaly head of the furry lizard, bending over it and whispering: Of course you'll inherit everything, I promise, psst, psst.

I close my eyes, the smoke swirls around inside my head.

Do you mean the actual suitcase?, I ask slowly.

You know what I mean, the old woman says and clears the cards away in one motion.

My real father?

You should leave now.

I stand, picking up the suitcase with a sigh, and pause in the doorway.

Who or what are *fairmen*?, I ask.

If you don't know, the soothsayer says, stroking the reptile's fur from its head to its tail, you will soon find out.

The storm has left. I make my way through the cemetery and look for the way out; I desperately need something to eat. I start daydreaming about roast chicken drumsticks with wild rice and gravy and small rounds of sweet carrots, and I wander ever deeper into a labyrinth of firs, weeping willows and square box hedges; past war memorials and tombs: penguins, elephants, naked young women gleefully sunning themselves, and, beside them, forlorn muscly men resting their exhausted heads on their knees. I stroke their toes, jealous of the ones they mourn. I go further on and calculate the ages of the dead from the dates on the gravestones, and I cry when I come across men who were as old as my father is. I observe the crows throwing each other nuts and I shuffle and hop and run along the gravel and drag and fling the suitcase high into the air.

In the bracken on the edge of the path, a thin, stone grey man is sitting on a plinth.

Hello, I say, brushing the gravel dust from the suitcase.

The man looks up from his book and regards me through his round spectacles. He has a pointed face and a moustache, one leg crossed over the other like a scholar. He holds himself contemplatively, propping himself up on his elbows, a cigarette held up to his cheek. A dried rose lies in his open book.

Hey, I say, I know you.

The man is silent.

I remember you being taller and, oddly, made of gold.

I sit on the suitcase and peer intently at the man, wondering whether he has blinked.

It's remarkable, I say, that I should meet you today of all days.

The man doesn't move a muscle.

Do you remember at all? My father and I, we used to come here every day to visit you. You were his idol. He asked you advice about his book, remember? I almost started writing something today myself. Then there was a mishap and I got distracted. What does it mean, do you think? Nothing? You used to respond to my father, we wouldn't have kept coming back otherwise. Maybe he still comes here? I'm actually looking for him to give him something. Would you like to know what it is? No? I think I'll wait here for him. He always had something to eat with him when I still knew him; sandwiches and cake and a thermos of tea – I swear I'm going to die of hunger!

The grey man listens to me attentively, and yet I have the impression that my visit isn't all that convenient for him.

Yes, I say, that's life. My friends are getting lines on their foreheads because the overhead projector is too far back and out of focus. I'm getting lines because I'm angry in my sleep. My friends study medicine and scrape fungus off of spleens because the corpses are rotting. And I do nothing all day long. I might as well be a statue: Girl with Suitcase, I'd like that. What about you?

The man on the plinth is silent and thinks, and I stay on the suitcase and try to remember what it was like sitting here in the pushchair while my father read and wrote next to me.

The wind rustles through the trees. I leave the cemetery, taking the suitcase with me.

The Fair Man

The road is lined with chestnut trees and never seems to end. I sit on the curb and wheeze. Maybe I could eat a bit of the kid, just a little finger, to stave off the hunger. I open the suitcase and immediately close it again. Then I yank up a tuft of grass from the edge of the street and gnaw on it. I lie on my back and look up at the sky. It's completely yellow.

Three grey Great Danes, big as calves, come walking down the street. They're nipping at each other's tails and snapping at motes and mites floating on the air. I duck down in the dusty grass, but the thinnest dog has already found me. It leaps straight at me. I want to get up and flee, but it's already pinning me down so I can't move. It rubs its rump around on my stomach and legs and pants at me from above. The dogs flap their flews and let the threads of drool swing like hammocks from the limp folds of skin. The largest dog dances around the suitcase, pauses for a moment, sniffs. Then it pushes up the lid with its nose. It looks inside and shakes itself so that its ears slap against its throat and skull. It eyes the kid in delight, noses and rummages around in the suitcase, and bites off one of the kid's ears.

Hey, I shout, hey –

Shut your face, snaps the dog on my stomach and bats at my face with its paws.

The ear falls out of the leader's mouth, it gives a barking laugh. Then it snaps it back up and gulps it down in one. It burps, the dog on my stomach howls, and all three of them laugh so much that their coats quiver over their bones. They can't pull themselves together, until they finally let me go and, still chuckling, and with their ears flying behind them, run off.

I sit up. A stream of people is coming up the road. I snap the suitcase shut, pat down my clothes, and watch them. More and more people step out from between the trees and into the road. They're wearing white robes with lace collars; the girls have wreaths of flowers in their hair and sandals with frilly socks on their feet. I join them. Snippets from a brass band float through the air, along with the scent of freshly mowed meadow and meatloaf.

The procession ends in front of a farmhouse. Clucking hens stalk around the yard, a calf with bulging eyes drinks from a trough. Red geraniums beckon from the window boxes. A girl is talking with a small, black pig.

The people gather in the front yard and whisper to each other. Standing in the doorway is a hulking woman with thick plaits looped around her ears. She's swinging a cowbell with both hands, and her plaits bounce plumply like smoked sausages. You have to get past her if you want to go in. She looks very strict, and the bell is very loud. The people are scraping their feet and plucking at each other's white collars. Some muster up enough courage to step forward and scream something in her ear. She drives away most of them with the bell, she lets in a few. That's when I catch a glimpse into the hall: there they are, at a great table, all eating cake. Flowers float in water glasses on the table. The children are crumbling up the cake and dunking pieces in the flower water, the elders fish them back out again. Some wolf down their cake in three big bites. They guzzle it down with cider. It runs out of their mouths straight onto their plates and when they laugh it sprays into the yellow faces of the flowers.

I sit on the suitcase and run my finger over the cracks in the leather, then suddenly there's a bang against the suitcase wall from the inside! I jump up and see the suitcase bulging out on one side. There's a terrible rasping sound, as if the kid is trying to roll over. I knock the suitcase over onto the ground and give both sides a firm kick.

Need some help?

A young man is blocking out the sun. I don't react, and stare stiffly and silently past him, so he shrugs his shoulders and turns towards the entrance, where the woman has just stopped ringing the bell. I subtly eye up his back, it is a nice back, you can see his muscles. A path of light blonde hair grows up the nape of his neck out of his shirt and leads up to curly locks that twine together like young serpents.

The young man abruptly turns and says: Looks like a good time.

Bright blonde hair sticks out of his chin. Does it hurt when the stiff hair grows? I used to wonder the same thing about my father. The young man makes use of two large, pale fish eyes. And there is a kink in his chin, I don't like that at all. He leans in towards me.

Are you hungry?

Yes, bloody starving, I say.

He looks astonished and laughs. His grin looks stupid and sugar sweet, as if cut right across his face with a knife. And he has chewing gum teeth, like a clay figurine.

Liver cake, trout cake, sweet cake?

Trout cake, I say, I want trout cake.

The young man nods and trots off to get the cake, I root around in my coat pockets. I find the cigarettes, light one up – almost very elegantly – and sit on the suitcase. I smile into the sun and think about the veins in the hand he had placed on my arm.

You smoke?

The young man is proffering a trout cake. You smoke!, he says. I don't like that at all.

Yes, I say, leering at his biceps, it's a way of life, smoking.

The young man doesn't say anything and looks over at the hill behind the farmhouse. The sun shines onto his mass of twining hair. A single hair is stuck to his chin, it gingerly wafts from side to side. I stand up to pluck it off, but then he suddenly turns and asks: Going somewhere?

Yes, I say, sitting back down. The hair has come off all by itself and is sailing to the ground.

Where are you heading to?, he asks.

To my father, I say. I'm going to see my father in the red city.

The young man falls silent again. His jaw muscles are taut and twitch like a horse's does.

It was very kind of you to bring me cake, I begin, if I could give you something in return I'd be glad to…

He stops grinding his jaw: What do you mean?

I don't know how to respond, and I'm suddenly worried about the kid again. I inconspicuously place my hands on the suitcase and feel for movement.

I mean, what have you got? He asks again impatiently when I don't reply. Perhaps you have something in your suitcase that I'd like?

I snort: I doubt that very much!

Maybe a little schnapps?

No schnapps unfortunately, I hiccup, oh how I would love a schnapps!

Pity, he says, stepping from one foot to the other, well then.

Wait! I shout, jumping up and taking the handle of the now motionless suitcase. You see that hill? We should hike up and eat our cake there, with a view. And see that kiosk at the foot of the hill? We can buy two large bottles of beer and have a good time!

Why not, he says.

We start walking.

We sit on the hill and look down at the farmhouse. Fish bones prick at my throat, I swallow but it's no use, they're really stuck. The young man sits in silence. I'd like to touch his fingers, I'd like to see if they're rough on the underside. I find calloused hands very attractive, I don't know where it comes from, after all, my father was a man of letters.

Where did this come from? I ask, gently touching his little finger with my index finger.

The nail is completely black.

He says: Look, it's already got a hole in it.

He stretches out his little finger very close to my eyes, and I really can make out a small hole in the finger nail. Sugar sweet. I quickly take a swig from my bottle.

Did you know, I say, that the dead bodies people cut up at the university go completely black after a while, too? They spend the whole year rotting, swimming in a soup until the students have studied every part.

No, says the young man, I didn't know that.

There you go. The dead don't care when you cut off all their bits and throw the skinned parts back in the pot to float around with other people's hands and feet and ears. That's what the students tell me anyway – what do you think?

I wouldn't know, he says, I'm not dead.

I'm glad, I say, I'm actually allergic to dead people.

The young man laughs. His teeth make me feel daring.

What do you think about children?, I ask.

Nothing at all, he says, I try and avoid them as much as possible.

Yes, I sigh, I should have done that too.

Do you have children?, he asks puzzled.

For heaven's sake, I cry out, no!

That's what I thought, he laughs again, I actually find children ghastly. Their shrill voices and their selfishness make me sick.

Precisely, I say, those little tyrants, I'd love to give them all a smack.

You shouldn't say things like that, retorts the young man. You'll probably have your own someday.

Never, I shout, fuck that! Those devils. They insult me, taunt and goad me till I bleed… –

I go silent. The young man squints.

Would you like another sip?

No, I say, no, thank you, I've had enough.

We sit in silence, and the young man inspects me from the side. I notice, even though I'm staring down at the house.

They're probably dancing, I say.

Probably, I say.

Would you dance with me?, I ask, I can put the suitcase in the corner.

Why not?, he says.

I pick up the suitcase, dangle it from my hand this way and that, and freeze. It's them! Slinking around the front yard of the farmhouse are the three terrible Great Danes, their noses in the air and their ears pricked. I can feel the kid thrashing around in the suitcase, I drop it heavily on the ground and sit down on it.

I can't, I say, I'm sorry, there's something I have to do.

What's up with you, the young man asks, are you not well?

He says it very quietly, he must be worried I drank too much because of him.

I place my fingertips on his arm. Then the air is ripped apart: lightning and deafening thunder, smoke, the farmhouse is exploding.

I look up at the sky, pieces are flying everywhere.

I've always wanted to see that, I shout and jump in the air, a house exploding – boom!

You're not in your right mind, shouts the young man, and flings his hands over his head.

Yes, I shout, and nuggets of brick clatter onto my skull, that's what my father used to say.

Flames blaze out the windows of the house. Through the blown-out hole in the roof the smoke rises up into the sky like a huge charcoal mushroom. People flood out of the door and cluster together in the yard. They shout frantically and look up at the roof. I squint, then stagger backwards – out of the smoke jump the three Great Danes! They gallop across the yard and up the hill. They're carrying fat sticks of dynamite in their mouths, I can see it clearly.

I really have to go!, I shout. The fumes in the air! I want to study one day – you can't study if you've ever had tuberculosis.

I grab the suitcase and run down the other side of the hill.

The Red City

I run the whole night, through fields and forests, always straight ahead, until I come to a city. I stop and look at the houses: blocks of red brick, unplastered and windowless, an iron bridge stretching right over the city; above it an empty sky, the moon a slice of lemon.

There are no lamps in the alleys. It smells of coal smoke and rotting meat. Skinned sheep heads hang over the doorways, mountains of rubbish and wrapped up, sleeping people clump together in dark corners. Suddenly a light flares up; a man in a hood stands in a doorway and sets fire to a scrap of cloth. He watches it for a while, the way it burns, then he drops it, and it goes out on the ground. The man turns to me.

Stop, he says, this way is closed.

I retrace my steps, but I'm lost. Cocooned figures huddle in doorways and hiss until I turn around and go down a different alley. I stumble over the slick cobbles, a cat jumps into my path. It's playing with something small, round, it rolls over the stones and gets stuck in a crevice. The cat pounces on it and gulps it down – ah! An eye.

I lie in a doorway on top of the suitcase and think about the young man. Something scurries past me, but I'm too exhausted to open my eyes. I soon sink into darkness.

A wooden cart rumbles past my head across the cobblestones. The midsummer sun shines straight in my face, the trout cake grumbles in my stomach. I reach for the suitcase and stand up.

The streets of the red city are now crowded with people and carts bearing parsley and huge slabs of meat. Whole pigs and cows are strung up out front of the shops, the butchers sharpen their sabres against stone counters. Half-dead mules trot past me frothing at the mouth, bales of cotton knotted to their backs, their swollen tongues hanging dumbly out from between their teeth. It's hot, a trail of coal smoke runs through the air that reeks of spices and piss.

At the edge of the street people are cooking live snails in huge cauldrons over a fire. The snails creep over the edges of the pots and burrow into knots in the wooden planks of the stand; people stand there pulling their steamed friends out of their little houses with toothpicks.

In a glass house fitted with rusty bars, men sit drinking tea. They wear long, white shirts, embroidered caps and all have moustaches. They take no notice of me even though I'm wearing a coat and boots in this weather and pulling a foul-smelling suitcase along behind me. Now and then, one of them takes a pull on a long, thin pipe. Their chairs are all lined up facing the same wall. The men stare at the wall and say nothing. In a dark corner a boy ladles slimy yellow soup out of a big pot. A second boy kneads dough and fries flat cakes in a pan, he coughs into his hand, then keeps on kneading. The men slurp loudly and smack their lips. There are only men on the streets; the women stand shrouded on the roofs and throw rubbish into the alleyways, where cats and the elderly wait to pounce on it.

The trout cake growls in my stomach again. I breathe in deeply, go to the barred teahouse and knock. The men keep on staring at the wall, only the one nearest the door wags his finger at me.

I'm looking for my father, I shout, can you help me?

The man hisses angrily at me, so I keep walking.

I turn off into a side street in the hope of finding a dark corner to rest, but there are some boys there fighting. Two flail at each other, a third boxes the air, four more sit against a house façade with outstretched legs shouting advice at them. One of the fighters pauses for a moment to scratch his stomach, then the other one yanks his ears, and the four boys against the wall jump up with a yell, flapping their arms.

I walk past them and hear them whisper and laugh. They run after me, and the biggest one blocks my way. He's wearing a yellow tracksuit, fraying grey at the edges. His nose is bunged up with dust, his moustache is patchy fluff.

Blocked, he says, you can't get through here.

The others stand behind him and snigger.

I hit the big one in the gut with the suitcase, he stumbles and falls on his back. The boys shout and jump at me, throw me down and, while I'm on the ground, pull at my clothes and the suitcase. It's about to open, I think, then there's the chime of a bicycle bell and the children fly from me and run to a cycling old man. They greet him and shake his hand, he ruffles their hair and says: Yes, yes, I like you very much. Then he whispers something into the ear of the biggest boy, points back down to the main street, and the boys wander off, but not without a bit of jeering and jostling.

Did you fall off?, the old man asks, and I sit up.

Then I see that he's sitting on a bicycle with stabilisers that he pedals by hand. He doesn't actually have any legs. His white whiskers are so well greased that they curl at the ends like a snail. He smells of jasmine and bitter old man sweat.

Fall off what?, I ask.

The man nods at the bridge standing large and black against the sky.

Sometimes they fall from it, he says.

My father lives here, I explain. He is a man of letters, he writes books.

The old man nods.

I don't know where, everything looks the same here.

The old man nods again.

Come, he says, just come with me.

The old man brakes with a screech in front of a doorway. In the semi-darkness inside, amongst pyramids of herbs and huge strainers, sits an old crone on a roll of gauze.

A man kneels in front of her, she's stretching out her foot towards him: an overgrown toenail has formed into a talon. The man has an enormous pair of scissors in his hand.

Come on then, whines the crone, cut it off.

The old man rings his bell and waves, and the woman with the claw waves back and tosses him a small can. The old man gives it to me, and I tug the ring pull. Inside it are pickled sausages that look like slender fingers.

You must be hungry, the old man says.

No, not a bit, I say, and the crone stretches her bony arm out towards me and fixes me with a fearsome stare, so I quickly eat one of the little fingers.

Delicious, I say, and she gives me a toothless grin.

The old man and I keep going. He has an air of pride on his bicycle, greeting people to his left and right, everyone knows him. Slightly bending forward, he peers at everything closely: figures in the alleys, feral cats, teahouses – as if it all belongs to him, as if he were surveying his city like a king would.

The smoke from the snail grills is unavoidable and clouds up around us. I stop walking and hold on tightly to the bicycle. The ground is shuddering, and the houses are warping. My head is awfully heavy, my fingers let go of the suitcase. I watch it fall to the ground in slow motion. Little man, I say and hear my voice as if from far away, I feel as though I'm falling apart.

My mother is cooking chicken broth. It's the only thing she can cook.

A fortifying broth, she says into the cabbage steam. I know you don't care for it, but it is a fortifying broth.

My mother has become even smaller, she just about reaches my nose. She scrutinises me with flitting eyes, her cheeks hot and red.

It's not that I don't like it, I say, I just don't want it every day.

If you cooked, my mother says, you could make whatever you wanted. But you always just put the gas on the highest setting and leave and don't come back.

I look out of the window. The wardens pace back and forth on the clay court of the institution. They have high green hats, which they tip when they pass a fellow warden or one of the inmates.

I saw a man today, my mother says, out in the yard. We smiled at each other.

Did you, I say.

But do you know what, he can't have been a day over thirty. I'm just not drawn to men of my age. They're so old! Somehow I've remained the age I was when I met your father.

I don't say anything, I stroke the pale chicken's back and tap my fingernails on its leg bone.

Have you seen your brother?, my mother asks all of a sudden. Was he at school today?

Of course, I lie.

I turn on the radio I bought from one of the wardens.

If she's not allowed a television, she has to at least have a radio, otherwise she'll notice that she's on her own, I told him.

The warden had nodded and stroked my hair. I almost bit his hand.

A sad song flows out from the fine silver grate. My mother pauses for a moment and sings along. *Somewhere over the rainbow*. She shakes the sticks of celery and begins to cut them into little half-moons.

The teacher called again, your brother wasn't at school today. I know it's not your job, but why don't you take better care of him? He's not doing well.

He's lazy and spoiled, apart from that there's nothing wrong with him.

My mother stops cutting and points the knife at me.

You sound like your father.

Not this again, I implore.

You're always on his side.

There aren't any sides, I say, I can think for myself.

The way you idolise him – it makes me sick!

Sorry, I say.

I'm all on my own, my mother says, I gave up everything for you both.

I know.

Your father didn't want children.

I know that, I shout, I've heard that since I was old enough to think. I'm alone too! My brother hates me, he's a monster and never listens to me. He sees the devil in me, the father that you've projected onto me. He left me too, why can't you see that? You're here with your head full of clouds, and I'm still the one putting my neck on the line!

You're so angry, she says wearily.

No, I say, balling my fists. Then it bursts out of me: Every night I dream that our house is on fire and I have to save my brother. Someone's trying to shoot us, a tiger wants to eat us, nuclear bombs are blowing sky high and he's so slow! I carry him on my shoulders, pull him along behind me by the hand, call to him that he has to run faster. I want to help him and I always lose him. Then sometimes I think that he's the one who set the bombs –

You know very well that I don't like onions, and yet you always put onions in, screams my mother and falls silent.

Lying on the chopping board next to the carrots is half a finger.

You've cut off your finger, I say.

My mother picks the finger up from the board and examines it.

I take the telephone receiver from the wall and call a warden.

They'll sew it right back on, I say, no problem.

The warden knocks on the door and enters.

You can sew it back on, can't you?, I ask him.

It's the same one that sold me the radio.

He guides my mother by the shoulders and says: we must be glad that life leaves traces on our body.

My mother smiles her weird, vague smile – I hate it: it throws stones in the sadness soup between my ribs. She puts the finger in the pocket of her apron. The warden leaves, and she goes with him.

I pick the chicken up by its leg, drop it in the pot and put the gas on the highest setting.

I wake up in a rubber dinghy. My father's lying next to me. The fair man from the cake festival is standing next to the boat. He has watched us sleeping and says: What's the difference between you two? You lie on your stomach, and you, like this, on your back.

My father paddles with his arms and says: That's because we have to swim all night!

I sit up, laughing.

The dinghy is in a living room. A dining room table is over there, and a dresser over here, on it a rusty teapot and a typewriter. The suitcase is on the floor by my feet, a pale green budgie is bobbing up and down on the leather handle and blinks at me with its head tilted to one side. I climb out of the boat and approach it, it flutters and hops over the floor. It's dragging one of its feet, there's a note attached to it. I catch the bird and release it from the papery burden attached with a rubber band. It makes for the window and flies off.

Outside there are high red housing blocks. Car parks and parched flower beds, decapitated palms, a small dirty swimming pool where tanned arms and heads are flailing. I press my face into the net curtains and sniff them. This is where my father is supposed to be living?

I unroll the message, *child support paid in advance* is written on it in my father's handwriting. It's wrapped around a thick bundle of banknotes. I hear someone coming along the corridor and pocket the money.

A pregnant woman stands in the doorway. She looks as if she's about to burst.

I'm Loribeth, I say, I'm looking for my father – your husband?

He's not here, the woman says and presses her hands into her lower back.

Where is he?, I ask, I have to give him his suitcase back.

He wants to swim in the sea, the woman says, not in the swimming pool.

I nod. She yawns and runs a hand over her taut belly.

It's kicking, she says, it's turning – she runs two fingers under her breasts back and forth – it's dragging its foot here.

My father doesn't want any children, I say. He never wanted children, he didn't even want me.

The old man is waiting outside the door on his bike eating sausages from the tin.

Well, he says.

He's not there, I say.

The old man scratches one of his stumps.

Three dogs came by asking for you. I gave them some sausages, they rolled over, all three of them. The children took them off to play.

Good, I say, that's very good.

The old man and I make our way through dug up streets, past tyre and motorbike shops, the suitcase in one hand, and then the other, until we reach the edge of the city.

Listen, the old man says, I know your father. He's waiting on the island.

What, I say, does he know that I'm coming?

No, he says, of course not. He dunks his finger in the sausage tin and sucks on it.

Even better, I say, then it'll be a surprise.

The old man shakes his head: you can't reach the island, no one leaves the red city.

He pours out the sausage brine and drops the tin, it lands in the dust with a rattle.

Then I'll go over the bridge, I say, I'm not afraid.

That won't work, he says impatiently, the bridge is like a rainbow, no one can find its end.

My father must have found it!

The old man laughs, bits of finger between his teeth. I start to cry.

Come, come, he says, upset, you're too old for that, there, there.

Where should I go then, I howl, sitting down in the street.

Now listen to me, he clumsily grabs my arm, I really know your father, he accompanied me on my walks and told me his stories. Would you like to hear one?

Yes, please, I sniff.

There was once a four-legged crow –

That's not by him, I laugh.

Then he's a scoundrel, the old man says, and we teeter onwards.

We come to a wide gravel path where a red flag bearing the image of a fist is waving in the breeze.

Place de la future, the old man says, spitting in the dirt.

Two gleaming automobiles are parked here twinkling in the sun. The red one begins to rattle and judder. The old man holds on to me tightly, we stand and watch. A quiet engine wheeze grows into a penetrating whistle. It suddenly rises up: the car zooms diagonally into the air above our heads, where it rotates on its axis like a tin spinning top. The pilot inside is being violently shaken about, his eyes and mouth wide open; he looks like he wants to come back down to earth.

I go over to the blue vehicle still resting on the ground. A man wearing flying goggles stares fearfully out of the window from the inside.

You, I shout, you have to be able to see from above: where do I find the beginning of the bridge out of the city?

The man in the goggles just shakes his head in alarm.

I beg you, I shout, pulling out the roll of banknotes and rapping it against the windscreen.

The door opens and the man in the goggles reaches out his hand, I high five him and he winces; I throw the suitcase onto the passenger seat and jump in on top of it. I pull a squashed cigarette out of my trouser pocket and hold it in front of the pilot's face. He presses his lips together, and I push the big red button for the cigarette lighter. The man with the goggles lets out a piercing cry. The car begins to roar and shake. We lift off into the air unsteadily. The distressed pilot casts off my hand, which I'd impulsively gripped around his arm. I open the door, throw out the cigarette, and wave to the old man down below.

I understand my father, I shout to drown out the noise. If this is the future, I don't want to live here either.

Me neither, the old man sighs, picking up the cigarette, believe me, me neither.

We fly over the city and brown mountains, their streets like a pencil drawn through butter. Black goats cockily stand on the summits and rotate their horned heads at the buzzing tin beetle – we wave to them. The sea appears behind the mountains. Spoon-silver and shining, it spreads out beneath us, the clouds are black on the horizon. The sun pokes through, shooting a beam of light onto the water, a rowing boat drifts through it –

The pilot pulls a lever, we start our descent.

Black dots are flying over the harbour: seagulls and the shoes of children playing ball; they're competing against the gulls at screeching. Three ships have docked: an old fishing cutter, a four-master and a tin ship smoking from its funnel. Painted across the boat's bow in big white letters is the word *ISLAND*.

Fridolin Seifert

The ship is made out of old tin cans, it smells of sardines and cat food. I put away my boarding pass (a yellowed and creased cinema ticket), stand against the ship's railing, and watch the harbour become smaller and smaller. The children jumping and pushing one another into the oily waves and swimming after the ship become tiny dots. I spit into the wind, until even the seagulls turn back. The waves rock the ship and spray my feet, I hold on tightly to the rail and rattle it. It's made from pink plastic and is absolutely not safe.

This'll do for today, I murmur, and pat the side of the suitcase. There's no response. My stomach rumbles.

I take a stroll. A board is hanging on the wall with *Bistro* written on it. A rickety wooden ladder leads down into the belly of the ship. I carefully climb down with the suitcase clamped between my chest and the ladder.

The bistro is circular and high-ceilinged, and the sun shines in through the portholes at the top of the room. There's an empty bar and round tables screwed to the floor. A young man is sitting in the sun at one of them, his face caught in its beams. He's wearing red shorts and a sunhat. His thin legs are planted in heavy boots.

We eye each other up.

You've got spindly legs, I say.

And you've got a big head, he says.

Your neck is too long, it's about to snap.

And you look like a fool because you don't have a stool.

I join him.

I'm wasting away, I say. May I be so bold as to tap you for some cash?

Very well, he says.

I can't remember the last time I ate. I could drop dead at any moment.

Preferably not, he says.

No, really, it could happen. Or someone might shoot me, just like that, bang.

Now stop that.

Well, I ought to tell you, I'm actually a criminal, I could be dangerous.

You seem pretty nice to me.

I am that too. But don't go getting any ideas, I'm already in love, very much so.

Let's raise a toast, to love, the skinny young man says, and passes his glass to me, don't mind me I'll drink from the bottle.

The young man is called Fridolin Seifert. He sticks his finger in the air and demands: Fish! A waiter comes climbing down the ladder and bows. He's a tall chap without any teeth, with a threadbare three-piece suit and a captain's hat. He has a floundering fish in each hand, which he kills with a well-aimed strike against the bar.

Fridolin Seifert narrows his eyes at his plate and tears tiny little pieces out of the fish. I eat far more ravenously and have already emptied the bottle of wine. Fridolin Seifert orders another.

You're not keeping up, I say.

The fish has grandiose yellow eyes, he says.

Give it to me, I say, I'm still hungry.

He slides the plate across the table and steals back the glass, swirling the wine: Tell me about your love.

I have a mouth full of fish and roll my eyes.

Is he rich? Sophisticated? A criminal, like you?

I shrug my shoulders: He's a fair man.

I understand, he says and stares into his wine.

It's probably already over anyway, I say after a while, I don't have any time for sagas, I'm on the run.

Fridolin Seifert buoyantly raises the glass, and spills a little wine: what a shame, he smiles, and chinks the bottle.

We drink. The wine starts taking effect. Fridolin Seifert removes his hat and slings it onto the floor. He gets up and unsteadily walks around the table. With heavy boot steps he climbs up the ladder to the deck, I climb up after him and watch him through the porthole. He's standing at the railing peeing into the sea.

You do realise, I shout, stretching my head out from below deck: that when the wind hits you it's spraying piss into your face. Lick your lips, you'll taste it.

Fridolin Seifert looks at me for a long time, then zips up his trousers.

I have to confess something to you, he says, and sways towards me. I love you very much.

The wind is so loud, I can't hear anything, I shout, and quickly climb down the ladder.

Shut your mouth!, he snaps from above, and jumps down. He lands with a dull thud, stands up and shakes out his feet. He stands in front of me, and pushes me to the floor by my shoulders. He says: Listen to... my... story. My mother had two white, tightly wrapped babies; they looked like cheerful maggots. One was smaller and had more curls and ribbons and lace around its head. It fell down, and its head turned to mush. My mother said: that's nature's way. She made a new one, and we all went to the funfair.

You're lying left, right and centre, I say, impressed.

And you? He asks, hiccupping.

I stand up and notice that the floor is swaying. I hold on tightly to his slim hips and try to look him straight in the eye.

Fridolin Seifert sighs: sleeping children are the sweetest.

This one isn't sleeping, I snigger.

No?

I look at the kid in the suitcase. A snail's trail of dried snot runs from its nose, the rings underneath its eyes shimmer like pools of petrol, and on its chapped lips are pearls of congealed blood.

Why does it only have one ear?, he asks.

It's a wild child, I say.

Fridolin Seifert reaches out and runs a hand over the kid's gnawed on collar.

We could take it out of the suitcase and raise it together, he says. I've always wanted a kid.

Are you mad? I laugh.

Just look at its little socks! He bats his eyelashes.

I take a deep swig out of the bottle and eye up the kid with my head to one side. It has really long eyelashes, I notice for the first time.

If it was wearing a bear costume, he says, you'd take it out in a flash. You'd carry it around and tweak its teeny toes. With ears and paws its eyes would instantly look so dear. Yes, if it was dressed-up as a little bear, you would take it out of the suitcase, and it would be your bear-child – ours, if you like, I would make it bread with honey.

Absolutely not, I say after a brief silence, it's already rotting. Children! Hanging off your arm, with drool over their faces, lapping up their own tears.

We could wash it and put it in a stripy shirt, he says with a twinkle in his eye, then we could take it to the theatre. And to rock concerts! I'll carry it on my shoulders and it will drum on my head, and when it's older it'll be a drumming sensation. You'll read it clever books, and it'll write its first novel at the age of five.

Seifert, I don't have the faintest idea what you're talking about.

I can feel the beating of my heart.

He tilts his head to one side and smiles broadly.

I wouldn't consider something like that for even a moment, I shout, and slam the suitcase shut, but he opens it again: We could teach it all the things we wanted to learn but can't anymore! Isn't that reason enough?

No, I say, that's atrocious.

Why are you schlepping it around with you then if you hate it so much?, he sniffs, rubbing his eyes.

Oh, don't be dramatic, I say and pat his cheek a little too hard.

It's not even mine. It's my father's, and I'm taking it to him. There!

I close the lid of the suitcase again, and Fridolin Seifert grabs the handle and holds the suitcase against his chest. I look at him, shaking my head. His arms sink.

You're a strange boy, Fridolin Seifert, I say and snap the gold clasps of the suitcase shut.

I'm a man, he says, and gulps.

Those are rather spindly legs for a man, I say, and climb up the ladder with the suitcase.

Through the porthole I see him walking around down below deck, taking off and putting on his hat, carefully putting the half-empty bottle of wine in his jacket pocket before slowly sinking to the floor against the wall. Now I can only see those hairy legs sticking out of the bulky boots.

I open the suitcase a crack and whisper: You horror. Did you hear that? Crazy Seifert had high hopes for you.

I look back through the window and say in a low voice: Stripy shirts! Bread and honey! And then there's those stork legs. I might have considered it with the fair man from the cake festival. But he doesn't like children – and I definitely don't.

I close the suitcase again. Suddenly everything becomes clear. I have to throw it into the sea. This Seifert is right: What am I doing? What kind of stupid idea is this anyway: chasing after my father to bring his belongings back to him? He could have fetched it himself, he could have visited just once, the scoundrel, where is this going to lead! Yes, dumping it is the only logical thing to do.

I lie down in the slipstream, put my feet up on the suitcase and roll my head back and forth with the waves.

Then I stand up, I want to get drunk. I pull the kid out of the suitcase and take it with me to the bistro. We sit at a long table, the kid carves notches in the wood with a knife. I buy everyone a round of white wine; I have to behave in front of the kid. I don't like white wine at all.

The kid has really got on my nerves right from the start, I tell a bearded man, I don't want to have to always take care of it. Don't you want to take it off my hands?

No, not one bit, the bearded man says, taking a large gulp of white wine, then he takes my head and clonks it against the wall.

I sit up. It's dark. Where am I? A bump is growing on my forehead. The ship groans and lurches. I must have rolled over the deck. I stand up and sit back down again. The wind howls and presses me to the floor, tiny suns are exploding in my head. The suitcase is gone.

The loudspeaker crackles. A man's slimy laughter rolls across the deck, there's the clearing of a throat, then tinny tones plink out the speakers, like the cranking of a music box. I recognise the voice of the waiter-captain from below deck, even though he's slurring and singing:

We are two mariners, our ship's sole survivors, in this belly of a whale –

The captain swallows, his cough cracks like a whip. The ship makes a sharp curve, I shuffle across the wet planks, my hands slide over the smooth walls, grip the railing. I call out for Fridolin Seifert, my voice drowns in the storm.

Its ribs are ceiling beams, its guts are carpeting, I guess we have some time to kill –

Where the hell is the suitcase? I pull myself up on the rickety railing, my hair flaps in the wind, I screw up my eyes: stormy waves, slavering white crests, torn open abysses, the looming clouds above break open black. The ship is going too fast, it flies over a metre-high wave and slaps – after a strange, soundless moment of weightlessness – like a stone hitting a lake at the bottom of a valley.

Don't know how I survived, the crew all was chewed alive, I must have slipped between his teeth –

The ship's now leaning to one side, water sprays in my face. We're ploughing through the waves, heading straight for the harbour wall of an island.

But, oh, what providence, what divine intelligence, that you should survive as well as me. It gives my eyes great joy to see your eyes fill with fear, to lean in close, and I will whisper the last words you'll hear.

I stand at the railing, once more looking for the suitcase. I can see the navigation bridge from here. I shout and wave. No one sees me. There's no one there. Then I jump. The water's really quite warm. The tin cans are smashed against the breakwater. I swim towards land.

The House in the Sea

The winter sun shines onto the beach and the pine forest. People sit in the trees and look out to sea. I walk past them through the sand. They sit in the trees in silence.

My eyes are dripping. The suitcase sinks deeper and deeper into the dark water, nibbled at by crabs and fish with grandiose yellow eyes. Flounders blabber, eels gape, the kid gapes back; morays wriggle, snapping at toes in stripy socks –

Seifert wanted to raise it, make it bread with honey!

And the sun sinks stately into the sea.

I will lie in the sand and sleep.

My father will come and carry me home. He swims in the sea and walks along the beach every day, that's his thing. Until then I'll lie here and listen to the waves digest the kid, tune in to the rolling and rumbling of the sea's stomach.

I dig my hands into the sand and curse the waves, they won't leave me in peace. They greedily lick at my feet; they have feasted on the kid, and now they want more. I stand up and hurl sand into their gullets; they rear up, frothing. They reach out towards me, towering up grey-black, sucking up everything in their path and crashing against one another. I run. The waves rise after me, grab hold of my feet. I tumble, shout for help, a whisper runs through the trees, but the branches are empty.

The water is already up to my knees when, out of the sea mist, a house emerges right before my eyes. It stands on stilts in the middle of the waves. They prop up two storeys: the bottom floor is little more than a skeleton without any walls, only a floor and ceiling with air and bare pillars in between. The smaller level on top is walled-in. It resembles the cabin of a ship, and gives the house the appearance of a little ark that, as soon as the water rises up, could ride away on the waves.

A platform runs around the outside of the second storey, its rusty railing shuddering in the wind. It could have been nice for walking around and looking out to sea, if it had ever been finished.

I stop and crane my neck, there's something alive up there: a bird is tangled in the iron bars of the railing. It's frantically flapping, it frees itself with a loud thwack and tumbles towards me. I catch it. It's a canary-yellow bathing towel.

I wade underneath the house between the stilts to the opposite side. From here onwards it's open sea, the water is up to my waist. A hole for a door has been left in the wall on the upper floor. A rope ladder dangles from it. I climb up.

Four heads peer out of the opening. No one offers me a hand as I climb up onto the platform. They just stand in the doorway tugging up their trousers. Notes are stuck to their foreheads.

I'm Loribeth, I say. The waves tried to eat me.

No one laughs. The tall one with curly hair buffs his glasses; he puffs noisily on them and smears the lenses with the holey hem of his woollen jumper. Another one with a knobbly, gnomish face gives a sheepish little cough and twists dried paint or egg yolk out of his beard. The third one has an angry red face, an unpleasant contrast to his garishly bleached straggly hair. His left foot is in plaster. He reaches out his hand and slowly removes the yellow towel from over my shoulder. A girl jostles forward and lights a cigarette. Her fine hair lies flatly against her head, and her ears stick right out. She gives me the once over, her eyes, beneath dyed pink eyebrows, run from my skull to my wet feet and back up again.

I don't want to ask, I say, but can I spend the night here?

We are in the middle of a game, barks the red-faced man, scratching inside his cast with the handle of a toothbrush. We may be some time.

The curly haired one shrugs his shoulders and nods.

Be quiet, the girl says, linking arms with me; I'll show you around.

Impossible, shouts the gnome, agitated, no one can abandon the game!

I'm a unicorn, the girls says, and removes the note from her head, it does in fact read *Unicorn*. She sticks it to the gnome's chest and leads me to the door. The boys stay outside on the platform.

Our steps resound around the box-like, windowless room. Only a little evening light presses shyly through the door hole, but the spotlights shining from the corners of the room cut off its path, throwing hard shadows onto the sketches on the walls, mostly squiggly self-portraits. On the bare concrete floor are six bathing towels laid out like beds, with cloudy water glasses and jam jars full of fag ends beside them. A clothesline is hung up straight across the room with prescriptions for cough syrup, sleeping tablets and sedatives pegged to it. It smells of cold smoke, wheat paste and spilled beer. The unicorn girl tells me something about the mould cultures they're cultivating here – they can't wait until they really flourish –, but I'm not really listening. I walk up to the only wall that isn't lit: three large oil paintings rise up from the floor to the ceiling and take up the whole wall. Colourful explosions: a mushroom cloud in the desert, a burning offshore oil rig, blown up houses in the middle of a city. I think of the burning farmhouse.

Who made these? I ask.

No one here, the unicorn says, and makes as if I should follow her. I stop again, this time in front of blurry photos of the four artists on the beach, having fun. There's one picture of Unicorn and the Curly One making out. Someone has written above it in pencil: *I'll love you forever.*

How can you know that?, I ask.

What?, she says and turns around. Oh, that was a long time ago. Come on – she takes my hand – I'll show you the best thing.

We sit on the edge of the roof and swing our legs. The waves roll beneath us.

Isn't it wonderful? Unicorn asks.

Not every contraction brings something new, I say. It just came into my head.

We smoke and flick ash into the wind.

Why do you live here? I ask.

Because no one else lives here, she says.

Aren't you afraid of the water?

It's OK, she says. I just can't go back to living with my parents. With their wasted lives, their lemon faces. When I look at them I lose all will to do anything, it makes me so depressed. You cannot resist it, the faces say, one day you'll be like this too.

Precisely, I agree.

But the waves are getting higher and higher. Last week they flooded the lower floor. We had our studios there, we're artists you know. She looks at me expectantly, and I nod. Now everything's in the sea, she sighs. We've got nothing left except each other, but what are we without our work? We're nothing without it, we're empty. We might act as if nothing's happened, as if these shoes and this hair still mean something, but what are we meant to wear them for? I've forgotten what we stand for, what we had to say, and starting all over again, no thank you.

We sit in silence.

Have you got a boyfriend?, Unicorn asks me after a while.

I have two, I say, one is cruelly beautiful, and the other is awfully strange.

You lucky devil!, she cries out.

Oh, the beautiful one got lost, and the strange one is at the bottom of the sea.

I'd like to have two boyfriends, she laughs.

I think everyone should be able to have two, I say, especially if they're so very different.

I mean, it's going well, she says quickly. But you never know what's on the horizon. You shouldn't meet the person you're going to stay with until you're twenty-seven.

And then you should ask to be shot, I say, by your best friend.

I was with someone once, Unicorn whispers, he lived here too sometimes. He always did so much thinking! But I learned: When you're in love, you have to enjoy it; at some point it's going to hurt no matter what.

I nod and look down at the flooded beach. A woman wearing a fluttering colourful shawl strolls through the ankle-high water. In one hand she's holding her shoes, in the other, her blonde boyfriend's hand.

I won't get anywhere here, Unicorn says.

She flicks her cigarette high up into the air and spits right after it.

Always the same stupid faces! I don't want to stay here just because I have him and want to hold on to him a bit longer. I'm still so young and have so much more I want to do!

She shakes my shoulder: don't you agree?

Yes, I say, looking back down at the beach. I hear the woman say to her boyfriend: I don't want to be with you anymore. And I see how a tremendous wave is rolling towards the land.

Unicorn pulls my hair.

Listen, she says, can't I come with you, please?

The gigantic wave reaches the shore and washes the woman away. Her boyfriend jumps in after her and goes straight under.

I quickly turn to Unicorn to see if she saw it too, but she's preoccupied with gnawing the black polish from her nails and sighing.

I stare into the water and think about Seifert and the suitcase. They'll all meet down below. The woman will ensnare the kid and Seifert too.

A wave spits on my feet.

The woman and her boyfriend haven't resurfaced.

Unicorn places a hand on my leg.

I'm so glad, she says, that you're here. It's boring with just the boys.

I begin to cry.

You know what, Unicorn says softly, stroking my hair, I lost a child once, too. It's bad today, but tomorrow you'll already see how absurd the whole thing was. I'll tell you about it: it was last summer at a party, we were pretty high on cough mixture.

No, I mean it!, I howl, fish with pointed teeth are tearing pieces out of it, right now they're biting off its little fingertips!

Unicorn presses her hand over my mouth and continues: we carried it around for two days and fed it and covered its ears because of the loud music – it was a girl. Alexander was the godfather, and we were smooching and suddenly she was gone. We ran around asking people: have you seen our child? We wailed, even Alexander. I fell on the grass and screamed: We've lost our child! I can't remember anything more than that, but we never found her.

The game down below seems to be finished, the artists are clattering around tidying up, calling for Unicorn, and climbing up onto the roof one after the other.

Where are the masks, shouts Eggbeard, what have you done with them?

Unicorn stretches out her empty palms towards him and says to me: We're nervous because tomorrow's a big day.

Shut up!, shouts Red Face and hits her angrily with his crutch.

She can come too, Unicorn shouts back, the more of us the better!

She whispers to me: We're starting a revolution.

For more freedom, Eggbeard says, suddenly standing behind us, and fixing me with his screwed up eyes, an uprising.

Oh, I say, great.

Come down, orders Red Face; he seems to be the leader. He points towards the rope ladder: Alexander and Una are coming.

We watch as a soaked-through young man climbs up. He's carrying the woman who was eaten by the waves on his back – they are the couple from the beach. And shoot me dead. It's the fair man from the cake festival.

Alexander, shouts Unicorn, blushing.

I look at the fair man's muscles – Alexander! –, the way they press against the wet shirt. My heart pumps in my stomach.

I stand beside Alexander on the platform and don't know where to look. Through the door hole I can see Unicorn towel drying the wet woman, who doesn't seem to be his girlfriend anymore, and who is utterly blue and dishevelled. I scrutinise his appearance. His clothes are shabby, I hadn't noticed before. Tracksuit bottoms with worn knees and the legs stuffed into holey woollen socks, a faded sweatshirt covered with flecks of paint. His face is smooth and a lot younger than last time.

You look different, I say, why did you shave?

He takes off his jumper and says: Why not?, in what might be an annoyed tone.

I stare blankly at his nose, trying not to look at his naked muscles, at his nipples, at the line of hair running up to his navel… I involuntarily touch his face, run my finger lightly over a scratch on his cheek.

Where did this come from?, I ask.

Did it myself, he murmurs, I scratch myself in my sleep.

He turns around and walks over to the artist boys, who are quietly quarrelling over the masks out of earshot of the girls. Now I'm outside by myself, freezing.

I watch as Alexander's ex-girlfriend tears the towel from Unicorn's hands and pushes her away from her. She pulls at her dripping clothes and screams: You've ripped off my work!

Eggbeard shakes his head and rolls a cigarette, Curly lets out a sigh, and the crutch-leader takes the mask from his head and laughs.

Watch out, he says, Una's going to explode.

Shut your face!, she screams. You steal my ideas, act all: Oh, what's this? I like that. I'll do that too. I'm the one who stands at the easel all day sweating! I do nothing else! But you want to have it all, you want to be artists and be cool! You want to be my friends, but maybe you're not my friends at all.

She points at Unicorn and Alexander, and her swollen eyes flicker with wrath: I've had it up to here with your lies, I'm not as stupid as you think. I'm leaving, then you'll see how far you get with your art. You dried-up, fame-hungry, desperate wannabes, devoid of the slightest talent – fuck you all! I'm going back to my father, it's nothing to be ashamed of, I'm still young!

She tears down the paintings of explosions from the wall, looks at what's left of them on the floor, and says more quietly: my father, who lies to me all the time, who says: You know what, Una, I really want to be famous again, and then just goes boozing, he just goes and gets drunk all the time, and says to me: Don't you go smoking cigarettes, you hear me, Una.

Unicorn has put her hands together in front of her mouth like she's praying, and Alexander is intently focused on the eyehole of the mask in his hands. The three artists stand up, take the exhausted Una by the arms, Unicorn skulking behind them, and together they escort her outside.

Alexander's bathing towel is grey.

He asks me to sit next to him on the towel.

Thank you so much, I say.

We're being kind and gentle, like children making up after a squabble.

Alexander lifts up the towel, beneath it are two squashed cucumber sandwiches. He holds one out to me, and we eat. He eats slowly and looks at me between bites; it's hard to say whether he's enjoying himself.

Do you want to fight it out?, I ask.

Alexander laughs.

I hardly thought of you at all, I say.

Really, he says.

We continue eating in silence.

The artists return without Una. They don't say anything and wander dejectedly among their artworks, scratching at the paint of their pictures, removing a couple of them. The leader lets Unicorn paint snails on his cast. Curly paints mould in wide circles on the wall. Eggbeard sits in the doorway and looks out to sea. The sun is setting. The red sky mixes with the glare of the halogen lamps. I become awfully sad.

I go out to the platform, where Alexander is emptying ashtrays into the wind.

I still haven't given you the money, I say.

What money, he asks.

You know, for the cake, I draw out the roll of notes, I'm rich now.

Alexander looks at the money. He turns around and goes back inside.

Child support, I shout after him, stolen from a foetus.

Shhh, Alexander puts a finger to his lips. Something's happening.

Curly walks around the room laying out a long cord. Eggbeard is leaning against the wall with his head bowed, Unicorn is sitting on the floor cross-legged with her chin held up on her fist. Once Curly has no more cord left, Red Leader stretches his arm into the air until his crutch touches the ceiling, and closes his eyes. Eggbeard pulls the lead for the spotlights out of the plug socket.

It goes completely dark. I hear the waves knocking into the stilts.

A light flares up; the leader is kneeling on the floor and is lighting the end of the fuse.

Fire burns through the curves of the fuse, it rustles around in a circle, spraying silver sparks; the smoke sneaks along sluggishly behind it.

We watch until the fuse burns out.

We wait.

Unicorn puts the lights back on.

Alexander snorts through his nose.

Eggbeard climbs onto the roof, a cigarette in his mouth.

Curly slowly follows the trace of the burning fuse over the floor.

The leader lies on his back.

I tap Alexander on the shoulder and whisper: Do you think I'm stupid?

It had been going around my head for a long time before I said it out loud.

He looks at me as if he's already forgotten I was there and says: Why?

I know so little, I say, I want to know everything. But I waste so much time on other things.

Maybe you're just too honest with yourself, Alexander says, and looks at me with serious eyes like pools full of sky.

Is that not important? I ask astounded. What's to become of people who aren't honest with themselves? Maybe something like what's been going on here?

Alexander hisses: At least they're doing something! All art is an expression of one's self, and I admire that.

Even if it's melodramatic and bad?

He doesn't answer.

I hate idealists, I say loudly and sneer in his face. I'm about to explode. I don't say anything else. He fumbles with his small, black fingernail.

I know a guy, I say, whose fingernail went black and then his finger fell off.

It's night-time. Alexander is on the floor doing press-ups, the artists are on the roof grilling a fallen seagull. I feel terribly alone. Seifert is dead, and the suitcase is gone. We could have been a happy family by now, playing cards and picnicking on a steamboat – if only I'd been brave, just this once.

Alexander hates children. I've met him again because I lost the suitcase; I willed it to happen. I watch him doing press-ups, and I despise him more with each one. His face is doughy, and his mouth opens weirdly. I see the vein in his neck bulge. I want to press it, jam the blood; it's all stirring within me. The thought of him scratching his face! These fine, dried traces of blood on his skin, they go straight into him, that's where he's breaking apart, that's where I want to go! I want to attack him, wrap myself around him, tear at his ears, munch on his hair.

Alexander, I say, you never pay me any compliments!

You're gorgeous, he pants. The blonde fuzz on your cheeks –

Good, I say, I'm going to sleep beside you tonight.

Alexander's kisses are like the kisses of a snake, and his breath smells of cucumber sandwiches. The floor is hard and my hair is sticky. Alexander snores. I huddle up close to him, it's cold; the wind whooshes with open arms up from the sea through the missing door and over our prone bodies. A crack runs across the floor, it runs directly underneath our towel. I listen to the breaking waves and the railing up on the roof and pray that the house won't collapse.

Fridolin Seifert climbs out of the water and points a gun at Alexander. Let's play a game, he says.

They saw for a bet, one log each; this is the game, I'm the prize. I'm wearing Alexander's old shirt with nothing underneath. Seifert wins.

Lori, now you belong to Seifert, Alexander says, and leaves.

Seifert is wearing a dog mask and shoots me with the gun. I don't die, even though I must have taken three shots to the chest. Blood bubbles out, my heart has been hit, everything has been hit, and I say: Ha, I won't die. And he shoots me again, and everything goes black.

It's already light out. The seagulls are screeching. The waves are quiet.

Alexander has rolled over towards me, his mouth is slightly open, a puddle of drool is pooling on the towel. I stroke the sweaty hair off his forehead and kiss his small black fingernail. Then I sneak over the artists rolled up in their towels and climb down the rope ladder in the gleaming light.

The sea has flooded the land, it's licking at the patch of sand, which is becoming smaller by the second.

The New Family

I sit on the wall in front of the supermarket and wait for my father. The shop is charred after a fire. The windows look like eyes with singed black brows. The whole city is smouldering; cars puff silver fireworks out of their smashed windshields, bins melt in thick black smoke. I would have liked to have been a part of it: the police dropped their shields and shrieked orders at one another, and the artists ran away, laughing. But they never asked if I'd like to join them.

But now, it's quiet again. The police are cleaning the streets with cloths and buckets of soapy water. And everything's on offer at the supermarket. Streams of people emerge from the darkness and form a queue. They come out with full shopping bags, twelve-packs of beer and crisps. They're carrying several bags at a time – now and then one rips, or someone loses their balance, and frozen fish and sausages roll over the ground, where they're eagerly gathered up and stuck into pockets by people springing out of the queue.

My father likes it when there's something going cheap. He buys a year's worth of tea and hot chocolate. He slinks around the aisles until the lights start flashing and one of the shop employees yells into the megaphone that everything will be another fifty percent off for the next five minutes. When he used to come home after these discount days, my brother and I would build towers out of cocoa and tea tins, while he sang opera and cooked in the kitchen.

My father shakes out the bedclothes every morning very thoroughly so that the pillows and duvet are fluffed up and have an airy scent in the evenings; after Alexander's fishy towel I'm looking forward to this most of all. If he really is on the island, then he'll come, and I'll sit here and wait. My father and I will sit together at the kitchen table and drink tea, I'll tell him about the artists, the old man with no legs, Alexander and Fridolin Seifert, but it's probably best not to mention the suitcase. We'll become misanthropic flatmates and will fill cracked teacups with seawater to breed crabs in.

I sit there swinging my legs, and at some point the shop closes, and the crowd of people disperses.

It's night-time, the street is submerged in orange light. Every now and then someone walks past me with a bulging shopping bag, probably for their family waiting at home where candles burn in the sitting room and soup is spooned out of ornate bowls.

I imagine following a man into his apartment. His hair is a little thin, but he has a huge bookcase in his living room, and it smells of wood. And there are golden candlesticks and a gas hob with pans filled with the leftovers from lunch. In one of the rooms is a wall decorated with world maps, and a little bed. He lives separated from his wife and has one child, who comes over every few days, a clever, quiet child who reads a lot and makes up stories. He likes the child a lot; when it's there, the three of us sit around the record player, listen to piano concertos and watch the record turn.

That sure would be nice, but no one else comes, no one else walks past.

On the opposite side of the street is an ornamental garden gate overgrown with hedges. A woman has been peering through it for some time. She looks left and right, then she waves at me, again and again, she wants me to come over. I stay seated for a little while longer, then I slide down from the wall and stumble over to her, sniffling.

Behind the hedge is a white house. A few people have gathered in the front garden and are craning their heads towards the house. I look very carefully at their faces trying to see if one of them is my father. Someone takes me by the hand and says: you've got to see this. He pulls me to the window, a woman is screaming inside. I'm lifted up and look into the living room – the people start cheering: it's a miracle!

They jostle for position beneath the window, pushing down each other's heads; everyone wants to see how the woman in the house is pushing a person out of her body and screaming because it's ripping her apart.

Breathing heavily and with my heart racing, I go back out into the street. A lamp shines above me and a moth sizzles against it, over and over again, until it's completely burnt up. I feel sick, but I have nothing in my stomach, the wretched cucumber sandwich has long been digested. I bend over and retch. A long, thin thread of spit slowly sinks towards the curb.

My head is about to burst, it resounds with words: Your birth was the most beautiful moment of my life... Blood and shit spraying everywhere... Your father didn't want to come, he wanted to finish his tea, I was already in labour… Not every contraction brings something new…

Overlaying the voices in my head is an image of powerful doctors' hands holding up a smeary, cramped crab, and the fine, slender fingers of my father with scissors in his hand.

Just as the slimy thread of saliva finally hits the ground, someone pokes me in the back.

Well, well, I hear, *ça va*?

The three Great Danes smirk down at me in the light of the streetlamp.

I see that I've grazed my hands from falling over and I want to get up, but as I try a thick paw shoves me in the chest and pushes me back down to the ground.

The leader shakes his body, his ears flap. I notice that they all have scratched noses and one of them is missing half an ear. I think of the boys in the red city, and try not to grin.

You think it's funny, drools the Great Dane with the tattered ear and makes as if to go for me, but the leader punches him on the muzzle. It looks me straight in the eye.

Where is the suitcase?, it asks.

She lost it, barks the other one.

The third one bends over my chest and sadly lowers its jowls. Slobber drips onto my face.

Such a shame, the leader sighs. We already have one ear, we just need the other one.

Eating ears, eating ears, the other two chant and do a little dance, while the leader leans forward and snuffles at my ear. I shake my head from side to side, and it roars: Shall I rip off your ear or your whole face, eh?

I close my eyes, its tongue licks my face, I feel the warm, stinking dog breath on my neck. The screech of car tyres – I open my eyes and watch the dog being thrown off me – a hand rushes towards me, grabs me, I fly into a car, and we speed off.

Fridolin Seifert is wearing a paper moustache and grins at me. The blonde girl at the steering wheel draws her head back in through the window and throws a victory sign. Then she slings her arms behind her and feels my face with both her hands while steering with her feet. Seifert leans over, pulls her fingers off my face and shouts: Stop showing off!

She laughs and I gasp: Seifert, you stole my suitcase!

Nah I didn't!, he beams and passes the suitcase from his lap to mine, I saved it. Like I just saved you.

Shut your gob, brother!, the girl says, her hands back on the steering wheel, you didn't do anything.

She turns her head and winks at me conspiratorially. She has a nose ring like an ox. And a moustache, a real blonde Viking moustache. Seifert sees me staring at her. He shrugs his shoulders and giggles. I push him against the car door. His sister pushes a cassette into the radio. A man sings about the war. I've never heard anything so wonderful.

I sit between Seifert and the suitcase, we race through fog and columns of lamplight, Seifert's sister stretches her palms flat against the roof and yowls along with the cassette man like a randy cat. Seifert joins in, and I take a deep breath and howl too, until I'm hoarse. I alternate tapping on the suitcase and on Seifert's knee, a daft grin on my face.

Fridolin Seifert and his sister have a wee in the dark. She looks like a rock, and he looks like a tree. I pat the flank of the car like it's a horse. Then I climb back in and quickly open the suitcase. The kid blinks. I blink back.

We drive around the island the whole night, and I wake up early in the morning. We're in a fishing village. I wind down the window, salty kelp air whirls inside, and I hear the fishermen shout excitedly in the harbour. They've caught a little whale; I can see it swimming in circles in the harbour basin. A fisherman is making whale noises, and the whale swims so close to him that he can pat its head. Suddenly he grabs it and lifts it out of the water – the whale is now a naked young man. He wriggles and tries to cover himself with his hands. The fisherman dunks his head underwater, then he pulls him back up by the hair.

Did you see that, I shout, a whale-man!

Ramshackle boats sway in the harbour, fishermen patch up their nets and scrape the scales from the fish; the whole ground crunches with glittering fish scales. Seagulls circle over the fish gutters and dive for a piece of skin or entrails. When they've guzzled down enough, they soar motionlessly against the wind and close their eyes. The harbour basin is empty. I ask a young fisherman washing out bloody buckets about the whale, but he shakes his head. I go to the next one, who is standing behind a mountain of piled up fish. He grips hold of them, one after the other, slitting open their stomachs with a big knife and ripping out their yellow guts. He cuts off their heads and pops their eyes out of their faces, they jump onto the table and the floor.

Come on, Lori, Seifert says, yawning. He cradles the suitcase as if it's an infant. No one saw the whale-man, you dreamt it.

We walk down a long, dusty street. Seifert's sister has taken a hacked-off swordfish head from the harbour and is slicing the air with it. She sings a pirate song, the sword swings dangerously. Seifert is walking a few steps behind us, telling the suitcase stories.

He's crazy, that Seifert, I say, he's completely mad.

His sister stops walking and throws the fish head at my feet.

You know what, she says, I had a baby once. My parents took it away from me. They live in a different city, I don't know where. One day I came home from the cinema, and in the cradle, where the baby should have been, was a note saying that it was gone, the child. I know for certain that my parents took it out of bed, and that father drank a cup of coffee while mother packed the baby's clothes. There were clothes missing, you see, and there was an empty cup with coffee stains in the kitchen sink.

A terrible story, I say.

Yes, the girl says, coating the fish head in the dust with her feet, he didn't even bother washing up the cup.

That really takes the biscuit, I say.

Fridolin is alright, she says, he just likes children.

Isn't that weird?, I ask.

No, she says, it's completely fine.

I think about it and say: He's already got thin hair. It would feel like I was close to death if I attached myself to someone like that. This bare patch at the top of his head, it's a constant reminder that nothing good ever lasts.

Yes, the girl with the moustache says, luckily I still have a lot of hair.

We come across a market. We make our way through the beggars, one of them grips my arm tightly and says: I'm not a thief, I don't drink wine and I don't take drugs. I just need two coins to buy a bratwurst.

I give him the money and he says: If you give me just one and a half coins more I can buy a mineral water.

I find this too brazen and don't give him any more.

Everyone's so poor here, Seifert's sister says and blows her nose into her hand. She wipes it down the awning of a stall selling hand-knitted baby socks that Seifert is looking at. I go with her to a girls' stall and we paint each other's faces with coloured rocks. Then I buy her a new nose ring; it's huge and has a molar tooth hanging from it. The vendors rub their hands with glee, they try to sell us roots and magic flour; we buy sweet woods and pickled olives and finally come to a stop in front of a stand with a tiger's pelt hanging from it. The vendor strokes it and bares his nicotine-stained camel teeth.

How much would you give me for it?, he asks, jangling his money bag.

Twenty five, I say, and spit out an olive stone.

Twenty five, whinnies the seller, no chance!

Very well, I say, thirty.

My esteemed young lady, this is a real tiger, I personally shot him myself, I'd keep it if I could, but my poor little daughter, home alone locked in her playpen, is hungry – for the sake of my misfortune, won't you give me fifty?

He massages his money bag, he even sniffs it.

I'd love nothing more than to pay fifty instead of thirty; yes, I can see that you are a dear man who practically gives away his wares out of pure human love –

That's how it is, the vendor cries out, all this misery comes from my accursed good nature.

You see, I say, I'm actually miserable too. But I could add an extra five on top.

The seller rocks his head from side to side: how about you put another five on top of that?

Adieu, Sir, I say and take Seifert's sister with me.

Just two more, the seller says and hobbles after us, two more? Ok, thirty, hey, come on, thirty!

I pause for a long time at a stall selling roast chickens. I lean over the counter and speak with the hens, stacked in cages against the wall watching as their pals get plucked, slaughtered, cut up, roasted and finally torn to pieces by rotten human teeth. The cage doors are open, but not one of the chickens dares to leave, they'd be next, they say. They play a game instead, but I don't understand the rules.

Right at the end of the market a wizened old man sits under a parasol selling mountains of teeth. There are incisors and canines and molars and wisdom teeth, some are broken, some have cavities. Next to the mountain of teeth are a row of neatly lined-up pink dentures with real yellowed teeth.

Have you got any ears?, I ask.

The old man nods and points to the dentures.

I buy one and give it to the kid in the suitcase.

Well, I say, one can make do with only one ear.

I find Seifert and his sister wrapped in the tiger skin, smoking by a cliff. Behind us they're dismantling the stalls, beneath us is the flat sea. The gulls squat in the water like spots of mould on old meat.

Seifert fixes his gaze on the suitcase, which I've set down beside me.

Careful, he says, it might fall over the edge.

I reach over him for the cigarette his sister is holding out towards me without replying.

Wonderful, Seifert says, a wonderful view, clean air.

His sister giggles and blows out some smoke.

It'd do the kid some good too, he continues, let's take it out so it can see the gulls and the sea.

Right, Seifert, now that's enough, I say, the kid is fine where it is in the suitcase.

Go on, let him, his sister says, it could do with some fresh air.

I stand up, shaking my head, and walk along the cliff edge, looking down at the quietly spraying sea. When I turn back, they've actually sat the kid between them. It has its head lying against Seifert's shoulder, and his sister's laughing about something or other.

I hear her shout: Fridolin, it smells disgusting!

And he says: Rubbish, that's just me. Look how nicely it's sitting, how peaceful it is. Oh, it smiled, it did, I swear!

Put it away!, I shout, come here, I've found something.

A steep path leads down between the rocks; stones come loose under our shoes, and we hold on tightly to the brushwood so we don't fall and smash ourselves against the cliffs. Out from the little houses growing out of the mountain come little bent old women trying to entice us inside. Their little houses have brown drapes and gardens with mossy tiles, but one of the old ladies is so nice that we stay for coffee.

The television is on in the old woman's living room, and dust bunnies are playing on the fitted carpet.

Seifert comes in from the kitchen with a plate of crumbly biscuits and sits himself down next to the old woman; his sister pats the woman's hands and calls her Nana.

It is so difficult, I hear the old woman sigh, while I watch the Tummy Buster advert on the television and scrape the bitter coffee fur from my tongue with my teeth, to keep a house in order at my age. If only someone would buy it, then I could go live with my sister in the city.

Seifert looks at me with his puppy-dog-hit-by-a-car eyes. I snort and quickly blow on my coffee when I see the old woman look at me confused.

Lori, Seifert's sister says, rubbing her yellow moustache, how much money do we have left? She reaches into my jacket, pulls out the remaining child support and says: We could buy the house, what do you think?

Seifert jumps up. We absolutely must, he shouts. A house! With a garden to plant vegetables in – a play area, a fireplace, a rabbit hutch!

He grabs the old woman by the hand and swings her around the living room, then lets her go and buzzes like a poisonous wasp around the house, taking measurements with his fingers and squinty eyes, muttering to himself.

I don't know, I say.

The house is the epitome of my domestic nightmare, but I can't say that. I finally say: I'm allergic to carpets.

Lori, Seifert shouts, running in, we'll just rip out the carpets. We'll put some handsome laminate flooring in! Quick as a flash!

I feel dizzy, and I go out into the garden. I look out to sea and try and breathe with the waves. I can hear Seifert and his sister squabbling about drilling holes and plug sockets inside.

The old woman walks through the garden gate and comes to a stop behind me. She takes a drag on a cigarette, her lungs creak. The smoke flutters down to the sea.

What is that, I ask, far out, like a shadow on the water?

The old woman screws up her eyes and a rattling whistle comes out of her.

It is so clear today, she wheezes, you can't usually see it. That is the island of fleeing fathers.

I take the suitcase from the living room and press the money into Seifert's hand.

I say: Rip out the carpet, but no laminated flooring, I want a real parquet floor. Make a start without me, I have to do something first.

I stumble and slip down the slope, the suitcase breaks my fall, and I say: Now we've got it, kid, now we've found him. Don't be sad, father's brilliant, you're going to have a great time.

On the shore I give a toothless fisherman the false teeth from the market and he lets me take his rowing boat. I row for half a day and land on a small island. The birds make a din. The sea churns the pebbles. The wind whips the palm trees. There is a house.

The Father

Father sits at the table with a pot of tea in front of him. He reads a book with a furrowed brow and taps a pencil against the tip of his nose. The green budgie sits next to him in a cage and sounds a whistle. My father looks up, blinks myopically in my direction, and a foolish expression spreads across his face.

Are you pleased to see me?, I ask, and hug him.

He won't let me go, I think he's crying.

Have you seen your brother?, my father asks as we both sit down at the table.

My brother!, I shout. Why does everything always have to be about him!

Why do you say that?, he asks, disappointed.

I could strangle him, I say.

He was such a sweet child.

So was I, I say, and then: He's just as unbearable as ever. Hangs out with his gang. His little friends adore him, and he's got a girlfriend now too. He's doing well.

Wonderful, my father says, suddenly looking sad, wonderful.

My father, my ageless, boyish father who looks so defiantly hard done by in his wedding photos, now has silvery hair and lines on his forehead.

I brought you something, I say quickly, do you want to see?

I'll make tea first, he says, standing up, this one has already gone cold. I've become a professor who is constantly making glasses of tea, always setting them down somewhere and forgetting to drink them.

So, I say, while my father spoons tea leaves into the pot and steam begins to rise from the water, what are you up to here?

He shrugs his shoulders.

I met your wife, I say, the pregnant one.

I see, he says.

In the red city, I say, in the rubber dinghy.

She's totally nuts, he blurts out. She lies around all day in the rubber dinghy, watches soap operas and stuffs herself with tins of pickled fish. In the evenings she goes completely loopy and throws my favourite tea glasses against the wall.

That's nothing new, I say, I know you like it.

She broke the needle on my record player!

Anyway, I took the child support money you sent her.

His brow furrows.

Alright, he says, then, what does it matter.

We sit in silence.

I have dogs now, he says, as my substitute children.

He smiles sadly.

Don't act like that, I say. You never wanted children. You just wanted a girlfriend, no children, you always said that.

So what?, he says. Then I actually had children and I loved them.

So what!, I shout. When you were taking us on a holiday you were so afraid of us you stopped the car in the middle of the motorway. You got out of the car and ran into a field. We watched you throw up into the crops.

That was the drugs, my father says, they call them flashbacks.

I know what they're called, I say defiantly.

The world doesn't revolve around you, he says.

You really have no idea, I say after a stunned pause.

Obviously, he says, suddenly very angry, and what about you? You act like it's normal to run off and leave your children.

My father stirs his tea in silence.

When I learned to tell the time I got my own watch, one for children. There was a clown on the clock face, his arms were the hands, do you remember? Every evening I waited behind the front door and stared at that stupid clown and his rotating arms – you always came home much too late. And I would feel sick with worry; I knew that one day you wouldn't come back.

That's not how it was at all, my father says.

You couldn't understand why I was angry; while you were out you forgot all about me, but I thought of nothing but you from the moment you walked out the door, scared that you'd be run over, mugged, or just vanish. Sometimes I would open the door, secretly loiter on the landing and listen for the door downstairs, listen for your carefree whistle. At some point our neighbour also started whistling, did you even notice that? And when you would come up the stairs and see me, standing on the landing biting into the bannister with a crumpled face, you would just press your discoveries into my hand – lemon verbena or roses, an injured bird – and say: I was only out for a stroll.

My father gives me a peculiar look.

Do you know, he then says, what I've been thinking about here, alone, on this island? Our thoughts are never free, they're constantly being determined and skewed by pre-existing patterns and habits. Try not to think at all! Our heads are full of flying scraps of rubbish that never let us think clearly. If someone succeeded in tidying these up, to blow them away and free themselves from these clichés of thought, our way of thinking would be different, and thus how we behave too.

I sigh.

For example, he proceeds, this humming or whistling of a song that automatically starts playing in my head in certain situations, like when I enter the university on the way to the lecture theatre for instance, it must be some kind of defence mechanism.

Coming home to us was so awful, I say, that you immediately had to whistle.

No, it wasn't, my father says so determinedly that I'm taken aback, that was different.

I know what you mean, I say after I've thought about it for a while. I do that too when I think about something: as soon as I notice that I'm thinking I stop my thoughts and rewind them in order to try and think them again in a different, more beautiful voice, to express them in a better way. I don't get very far with my thoughts, because this conceited voice wants to stop, rewind and improve them over and over again, then I get upset and we argue and I end up completely tongue-tied. Do you understand?

No, he says.

We sit in silence.

The spoon tinkles against the glass and it sounds like home.

The bird sits in the cage and cleans its feathers.

My father gets up to watch it.

Every morning he hops about, flapping and tweeting so excitedly that I wake with a fright and think something's happened.

My father laughs: but he's just happy about the new day! That bird brain!

I put the suitcase on the table and open it. The kid is asleep.

I'll leave it here with you, ok?

My father grimaces.

I don't have time for that, he grouses.

You sit here the whole day drinking tea and reading. You can do all those things. It's yours, you know that.

But you're grown up now, he says, you could take care of it yourself.

I don't want to, I say. It's sweet and quite amusing at times, but I'd like to cultivate my own worries for a change.

Children always inherit their parents' worries, my father says. That's the way it is, so parents don't have to have them anymore.

No, I say. I have other plans. My boyfriend Seifert, his sister and I have bought a house, on the rock island.

You're moving in with your boyfriend? Into a house with fitted carpets?

Ha, now you want to give me advice?

He laughs. It makes me angry.

I could never rely on you –

And I could on you?

You didn't have to, I howl, I'm the child!

My father pats me on the head. That was my punishment when I was little. I remember that he only had to threaten to do it if I didn't want to brush my teeth or I had lost my shoes and I didn't want to look for them. I would jump to it out of fear of this punishment. Now this ever so gentle touch almost brings me to tears.

You've got a potato nose like your mother, my father says, harrumphing away the tender moment.

You always used to say that so I wouldn't become vain, I say. But someone swore, and very recently, that I have a small, cute nose; yes, he or she insisted that it was impudent how cute and small my nose is. Now, who was it?

Don't rock like that, my father says, and I stop moving my upper body back and forth. I do that, he says, and he actually is, just like I am, rocking back and forth, to the same beat.

Genetic, I exclaim enthusiastically, it must be genetic!

Nonsense, he says, it's another kind of calming mechanism.

Anyway, I say stubbornly, both of the Seiferts are the best thing to have ever happened to me, I want to be a family with them.

Well, my father says, if that's what you want.

And why not? I'm not like you.

You're very like me.

We laugh.

I mean, he says, don't you want to see more, experience more and learn more before you settle down?

I've seen enough, I say, enough for a whole lifetime. Now I could use a bit of happiness.

Happiness is for normal people, my father says.

He presses a finger to my forehead: don't goggle like that, you'll get wrinkles.

Nonsense, I say.

And if that's the way it's going to be, he says looking at me strangely, it's high time you thought of children isn't it...

I know he's making fun of me, and I say, just to annoy him: perhaps.

No! he exclaims. You think that the world is more bearable when you have a child because a child experiences the world differently – everything is magical to a child. But that's not how it is, you can't bring back your own childhood. You lose it more than ever and are then forevermore depended upon, shackled, under the yoke!

Don't exaggerate, I say, it wasn't that bad.

I was bored to death, my father says, pushing the pram up the same hill day in and day out, and you were always asleep.

Anyway, I'm leaving the kid here, I don't have any use for it.

My father looks at the kid and strokes its sweaty hair from its brow.

I keep having a dream, he says, of a tunnel. I have to crawl through it, and it overwhelms me. It's narrow and dark, and I can't make it out. I think I'm traumatised from my own birth.

He stares into nothingness, lost in thought, and I look at his growing belly, protruding over his waistband. He thinks that his honesty has brought us closer, but I don't know if I feel the same way. It's strange; things between us are like they used to be, but also completely different. How was it back then anyway? Aren't memories nothing more than lies of our own – and others' – making?

Evening comes, and I have to row back. I can tell my father wants me to stay.

I would, but Seifert and his sister are waiting for me, we want to begin our new life together.

Well go, he says, and gives me tea and honey and books that I absolutely must read.

What will you do now? I ask.

My father shrugs his shoulders, smiling lopsidedly. He shows me the book he's reading, it's called: *Thinking Clearly*.

And I'm not alone, he raps on the suitcase. And I have the dogs, he says.

Where are the dogs? I ask.

He nods towards the window.

They roam around the whole day, and when they come back they eat a whole week's worth of supplies. Then they sleep for two days and head back out again. They're quite strange companions.

Three calf-sized Great Danes, I guess.

Have you seen them?, he exclaims. They're a little out of control, they've gone a bit wild.

Yes, I say, they like the kid so much they could just eat him up. It would be best if you kept an eye on them from now on, otherwise you'll have to sew what's left of the kid back together again.

I have to mend the kennel door, he sighs, they keep escaping.

Father waves as I push the boat away from the shore. Next to him is the suitcase, and the three dogs dash about between the trees, trotting around them with flapping ears.

The Party

Fridolin Seifert washes up the cutlery and throws it onto the draining board with a loud clatter. He always washes the glasses first, then the plates, and then the pans he left to soak in the sink in cold water even before we've eaten. Only then does he wash the cutlery. It drives his sister Mabel mad: this whole tidying thing Fridolin has going on drives me mad, she says.

We lie on the carpet and play a game that we made up that afternoon. You have to catch the other's toe with your toes, that's the game.

Mabel has been wearing her white bathrobe and a tonne of gold chains around her neck for days, and I'm wearing light blue shorts and a stretched t-shirt with an ad logo on the front that belongs to Seifert. He's wearing what he always wears. His hair has got thinner, but you hardly ever see it, he wears a cap.

We could go into the city, I suggest, ogle the beggars.

Or go to the party at the castle, Mabel says, catching my big toe with her greasy toes.

Or we could just stay home, Seifert says, wiping down the kitchen tops with a cloth; water droplets from washing up, he says, and polishes them again.

He drives me mad, Mabel says.

Mabel has fallen in love and has been insufferable ever since. Every week she climbs into Seifert's boots, stomps out of the door, climbs onto a bicycle, a different one each time. She comes back on foot with bags full of out-of-date meat, a crimson face and pearls of sweat in her moustache. Then she throws herself down in a corner, and Seifert has to sing kitschy pop songs for her, and when he gets to the line: *And the space between the kisses like the length of our shadows*, she snaps and beats him up, until he cries. They roll around on the floor, while I stand in the garden in front of the fire and smell the meat. Sometimes I see my father's island light up in the sea, and then I think of him and the kid, how they'll be sitting in the kitchen reading. I stroke the cold meat and visualise how someone put every single cell into it and that's how the meat came into being, and then I lick it and hope that the dogs will come over the cliff edge into the garden on the prowl. And I think about Alexander and whether it would have been more fun with him, but I know that it wouldn't have.

Do you think it'll be any good? The party at the castle?, I ask, tugging on the cord of Mabel's bathrobe.

Yes, she says, no, I'm not in the mood to do anything.

The wind rattles the window, and the flowers in the garden have gone brown. They have to be pulled out so new ones can grow, but who's going to do it.

We've been in this house for six months now, lying on the carpet because we threw the old woman's mouldy three-piece suite into the sea and haven't managed to build our own furniture, like Seifert and Mabel said we would. He cleans and she reads thousand-page sci-fi novels and is unresponsive while doing so.

In the beginning I still tried to write, but that soon passed. What would I write? I'm no cleverer than I was before, if anything I understand even less. The greatest mysteries have become as flat as paper, unresolved, and yet no longer that urgent.

While Mabel reads I snooze or observe the animal shapes the mould forms on the ceiling. You can really lose yourself in anything; days go by spent pressing patterns into my skin with my thumbnail, snakes, beasts, tortoises; other days I listen in to the noises the house makes – the leaky tap in the bathroom, the fluttering pages of Mabel's book, the click of Seifert cutting his toenails. Often it's all too much. I feel woozy all the time, and when I lie down I fall straight to sleep. I tumble down into a dark swoon, then I wake with a jolt, hyperventilating, like I'm being suffocated, and stumble towards the window to suck in the salty sea air.

Let's go out, I say, and Mabel sits bolt upright: The main thing is we finally have some fun again!

The car comes to a stop in front of a castle, headlights beaming onto the façade. Mabel opens the door and runs out, she dances in front of the car lights, and her gigantic shadow writhes like a goblin against the castle wall. Seifert grips the steering wheel and honks the horn in time with the music flowing out of the castle. A rocket soars from the tower and bursts in the air. My heart is beating strangely.

Inside there are tables and chairs and a bar with a bowl of pasta salad. I stick my hand into it and mash overcooked, lukewarm pasta between my fingers. Mabel is already dancing with her girl, she's wearing a feathered eye mask, their arms and hair are flying around them, they pivot and shake and shriek.

Seifert and I sit at a table and drink beer. A child is asleep in a pushchair in the corner. Seifert looks at it and sighs. I look at his knee and think about how he sliced himself with the carpet cutter when he tried to rip out the fitted carpet. It had bled terribly, sprayed all over the carpet, but he just stood there stiff as a poker, staring. I pressed paper and old t-shirts over the cut, and while I felt his warm blood on my fingers and stroked his hair with my free hand, I thought to myself: this person doesn't have what it takes to lead a responsible life. I shoo away the thoughts and move a little, bend my leg to the beat and bounce my shoulders. It's as if I'm filled with sand. I look at Seifert's beer and at the smoke rising from between my fingers.

I say: Did you know that an octopus eats itself if it's starving?

It also has eight arms, Seifert says, without taking his eyes off the child.

He'd packed the striped shirts he'd bought for the kid at the market into one of the old woman's suitcases and put it on the TV table in the living room. That's where it's been ever since, and no one is allowed to move it, otherwise Fridolin has a breakdown, as Mabel puts it. That's when he hurtles through the house, cleaning everything, and Mabel and I have to sit in the garden so we don't get in his way. In the beginning we wanted to help, but he screamed that we would do it all wrong, so we went back into the garden and spat into the wind off the edge of the cliff.

Mabel comes rushing over and groans about how much the music is in her body and how much she can feel it. Then she tumbles back into the fray.

Seifert and I look at one another.

It's a funny sort of room this, he says, a funny room. There used to be a prison on the top floor. Now a monk lives here – the oddest person on this planet. He was a rebel and a bank director, and now he's a monk. He showed me the prison once, there's a draft in the cells, you can sense the vibrations, it's not very nice.

Full of ghosts, I say.

Yes, full of ghosts.

He looks back over to the pushchair.

Oi, Seifert, I say, pull yourself together.

He stubbornly falls silent, and I say with my eyes on Mabel: the others always have more fun.

He looks at me and says quietly: do you think things will ever be good again?

What, I say dumbly.

He mumbles something about beer and leaves. I stay sitting on my own and watch Mabel and the masked girl dance. Mabel notices and staggers over to me, she pulls me onto the dance floor and shouts: We have to have fun!

I wiggle a bit this way and that. The masked girl swings her breasts, and Mabel's nose ring flaps. I find them awfully goofy, and I find myself dreary.

I make my way up to the roof and look down. The walls of the castle are daubed with dirt and there's filth in the yard. Beer cans and chunks of plaster fly out of the windows, rockets whiz and bang. The castle seethes like a volcano: instead of magma, it's a mass of people that erupts from it, lost souls that have to dance so constantly and so hard in order to not get cold and petrify. They're exhaled out of the doors and windows, they stream out with timber beams and iron rods, hitting cars and trees and each other. They thrash themselves amongst the shards and the dirt in the bushes.

The girls come up, dramatically fanning air into their red, sweaty faces and sit down in front of the arrow slits. The girl with the mask rolls a cigarette and tells us how she's been cleaning her oven: three days of spraying and letting the chemicals take effect.

You're just like my brother, Mabel says, why did you have to marry that man?

Oh, come on, he's nice and he's a good cook, says the girl, trying to patch up a hole in the cigarette paper with her tongue.

Your most exciting face showed itself, says Mabel, every time you fell in love with someone else.

I have a big heart, the girl says and smiles at me.

She puffs a white cloud up into the sky.

Then she says: I can't believe it's going to be winter. I don't understand why it ever has to be winter.

I say: did you see the lamps have gone out?

On the horizon behind the castle the lights flicker and gutter. We smoke in silence.

I have wrinkles already, I say, here.

The girl with the mask puts her face very close to mine.

It gives you character, she says.

Then I'd rather not have any character, I say.

Mabel straightens her back and holds her head in her hands. She says: Since we've been living in that house, I've become strange. My eye twitches, and even when it doesn't twitch I've got used to screwing up my face in frustration as if my eye had just twitched. I'll stare blankly at my companion and not register even a jot of empathy wash over me. Instead I've started noticing how people poke about inside their ears, how they talk while prodding their finger nails in and out, how they twirl their eyebrows between their fingers, how they finger their nostrils and then rub their fingers below their noses so they can smell them better. They're all nuts, she shouts in a shrill voice. And everything's spinning inside my head. When will I finally arrive?

The girl with the mask puts her hand on Mabel's cheek and says: I have sleeping pills, they're highly toxic. Do you want one?

She places a tablet on her tongue and one on Mabel's too.

Delicious, she says, got any more?

The girl throws a handful of pills high into the air, they fluoresce in the sky, shining drug stars, we catch them in our open mouths.

Then we lie down and wait.

Mabel stands up and declares, slurring: there was once a boy, I gave birth to him, but I can't remember it all that well. I put him in a locker, wrapped up in a bath towel, I was afraid of taking him out, he didn't drink anything, he became weaker and weaker. He squinted and had a permanently frightened expression. Whenever I was almost ready to breastfeed him the school bell would ring and call me away. Mabel opens her eyes and imitates a shrill bell, then she carries on gabbing: Later on my mother called round, she was holding the boy, he was bigger and happier, a little dirty, I said: No mother, please keep him for a little longer. She said: No, you have to take responsibility for him. But mother, I said, I have to go to school. She said: you don't have to go to school anymore. Shit, it was actually true. I locked the child in a box because it got on my nerves, and while I was doing it my sewing box fell down and a thousand tiny pins tipped all over the floor, and I had to gather them together and I cried because it was so terrible. I slept a little in the child's room. Later, I let the child out again. It had become a wise old man. He was very understanding about me locking him up, and forgave me straight away, but it didn't make me feel better…

Mabel collapses.

I stand up and close my eyes. Music trickles from the sky, quietly at first, then rising in volume. Synthetic melodies, slow clapping, bubbling like when someone's drowning. I throw my head around and send my hair flying, I shake my shoulders and turn in a circle. At some point I see Mabel kissing the girl with the mask, and I go over and kiss her too. Her tongue is soft, and she uses a lot of lip balm. She's not wearing the mask anymore, and now I see that she has very fair skin and bright red hair and those red-rimmed bulging eyes sensitive red-heads have.

I have a sticky tongue from all the tablets and yet I cannot die.

You have to go to sleep, then you'll die, the girls say, and they begin to die.

The End

I'm the only one who sees the wave roll in. It swills around the castle, the foundations are already sinking into the sludge. The wind tears people and tiles from the roof and drops them into the slurping water. The girls and Seifert are gone.

I lie on my back and look at the sky: whistling meteorites, their tails spraying in every colour, it's a spectacular concert, the finale. I lie there and conduct:

Forte, I shout, *fortissimo da capo al fine!*

And suddenly, rising up from it all, is the fair man. Alexander, naked, golden flames dancing all around him. He's using a propeller and flies directly towards me. I stay where I am, smiling, I say: Alexander, Alexander, and he hovers over me. He hangs onto the propeller with one hand and pulls me up with the other; I wrap my arms and legs tightly around him. Glowing little snakes fawn over us, they're warm and sing quietly. This is how we fly over the sunken castle, over the edge of the island, out over the overflowing, foaming brown sea.

I'm not saying anything because I'm not speaking today, Alexander shouts. I wanted to say something stupid, but I'm not going to say it.

I look down into the thunderous water.

My father was a good swimmer, I shout, he was a whale after all.

You're a strange little bird, Alexander says, and blows in my ear.

His breath smells of baked apples, and his skin is soft like silken velvet. Underneath, it's as hard as steel cable. I wind my legs even more tightly around him. His face is littered with little bloody scratches... I grab his hair and bite his cheek, we kiss and slowly sink.

I rise back up alone, Alexander falls, lands on his back, is swallowed by slick black waves. I'm holding a lock of blonde hair in my hand. I let it sail down to the surface of the sea. Where it lands on the water, an island emerges. A glass church towers up out of it.

I land on the stairs leading to the church. It really is completely made of glass. The wings of the door noiselessly open all by themselves. I step inside, the door closes behind me.

It's quiet in here. There's a larger than life-size statue of the Virgin Mary in the entrance, she's surrounded by pointed silver beams. I smile at her and climb the spiral staircase until I'm right at the top in the bell tower.

It's a high, bright room, the bells hang from the ceiling. I place my forehead against the glass and look out: the waves are dark, the sky is black. It's only right at the back, at the back of the sea, on the horizon, that it's rosy-red and sallow-yellow. A wave rises and hits the top of the church, exploding with a crash against the glass. I draw my head back and slip under the largest bell.

Beneath it, wrapped in a knitted woollen blanket, is the old soothsayer.

The soothsayer smiles, but not as if she recognises me. She doesn't look well; her blue hair is matted and sticks out in clumps at the back of her head, her make-up is dried out and flakes with every twitch of her skin.

Where's your beast? I ask.

We all lose companions, she says hoarsely.

I try to give her a sympathetic look and say: I brought the suitcase to my father.

So, she says, what are you doing here then?

Dreary, I say, such a dreary life. I need a new path.

This is the end, the soothsayer says, exhaustedly, there's no way forward.

But that can't be, I shout, I did everything you told me to do – I even married Fridolin Seifert! A woman of the night wed us, she slept in our garden and promised to bring us soup. She never did. It's so dull! I always want to be somewhere else, never the place where I am. But what use is going somewhere else? I always take myself with me.

The old woman isn't listening at all, she's fussing with the wool blanket, and I shake her by the shoulders: There's a whooshing in my ears! I'm completely lost. I don't recognise myself in the mirror; this is not how I imagined myself, so lazy, vulgar and wicked. I don't want to be that person. The only solution that came to me yesterday while I was half asleep: to enter the square! To kill myself. And then the fair man saved me.

Fair men are a pain, the soothsayer sighs.

Yeah, yeah, I say, but what about the success you promised me? I have no life, no trade, no talent, nothing. I never manage to achieve anything for which I could be rewarded with success. Isn't that what success is: you do well and people are jealous of you? Because you've got a gravel driveway and drink tea on the terrace, and mosquitoes fall in the tea, and the wind rustles through the eucalyptus trees. But me, I mope around in the filthy, carpeted house with Seifert and Mabel, who only smoke, clean the fridge and watch TV until they fall asleep. A wall races towards me, and this wall is my future, it comes much too quickly, and crushes me. That must be how my father felt – can't we ever be something other than our parents?

The soothsayer looks at me with squinting eyes. Have you got any more of those pills?

I reach into my trouser pocket and pull out two crumbling, damp tablets. We take one each and hum ourselves into a soft, round drug hollow.

Behind the glass church is a silent cemetery. It looks like an estate of terraced houses, with wide gravel paths and old pines. The small houses have crosses instead of chimneys, they have golden locks and doors made of latticed glass. Small flower arrangements are jammed between the bars. I look in as I walk by. Inside are small tables covered in crocheted tablecloths with flowers and photos and candles and plastic statues on top. Small carpeted parlours where Mary and Jesus jostle for space with candlesticks. The dead live in these parlours.

Shelves are screwed to the walls, this is where the coffins are displayed. Some are covered with woollen blankets, so they don't gather dust or freeze; others shine in the candlelight like grand pianos. Entire families lie here, sleeping one above the other in bunk beds, on good terms with one another at last.

I'd like to have that too: a house with our family name above the door where people can come and visit us when we're dead. They could furnish it, the parlour, with objects from our lives: birdcages, books, teapots, my mother's radio, my father's typewriter, my brother's cigarette aeroplane for all I care. And something from me. And our descendants can come, if they miss us, come sit in the little house and tell us all about the new world, they can climb up the little ladder, sit hunched on the chaise-longue – like in the sleeper carriage on a train – pry open a coffin and see us sleeping and smiling.

I stand in front of a small, grey mausoleum, not much higher than myself, made of plain, unadorned concrete. The door is open, the windows are shattered, inside lies a coffin fallen from its shelf, one end on the floor, the lid open a crack.

I see myself in the reflection of the cracked glass: striped jumper, coat, a pale face. I wait for something to happen, for something to move inside, but it's completely silent, I'm the only thing that moves, me and my reflection.

I open the door and slip inside. I breathe shallowly at first, hold my hand in front of my mouth and nose, my heart thumping. I stand completely still between the coffin lying at an angle and the wall of shelves. There are no statues or pictures here. I take my hand from my face: it smells of warm wood and dust.

I try to see inside the coffin through the gap. It's a simple, unpainted box, the wood is already completely grey. I run my fingers over the paths and furrows in the wood. Then I open the creaking lid.

I climb inside, stand in it until it stops rocking, then I sit down, like I'm in a lopsided bath tub, I slowly lay my head back. I stand up again, climb back out, try to hoist the coffin back into position on the shelf. I take hold of the coffin and slide it up, back onto the shelf.

I climb in afterwards and lie down, close my eyes. It's completely silent.

The carousel begins to turn.

The house I live in with Seifert and Mabel looks different: it's bright, we have a parquet floor. I hear Seifert whistle lovely melodies outside; he has built a stage in the garden and is hammering at it. We're going to play today, Seifert on drums, Mabel on bass, I'm going to play guitar and sing. They'll come from all around the city, our friends, our fans, they'll cheer and clap for us. Around the stage are a tyre swing, a sand pit, a slide. Seifert looks through my window, sticks out his tongue and mimes affectionate kisses at me. Mabel stands in the kitchen and cowers from the smoking oven. Her girlfriend with the mask will be coming home from work soon, and she wants to prove to us that she can do something other than steal bicycles. I stand up from my desk and go to her, we cut off the blackened ends of the cake and burn our fingers. We put them in each other's mouths, smear it over our faces, and we laugh.

Lights out.

It's completely silent and dark.

The carousel creaks.

I wake with a start. Dark room, heavy breathing, now and then the sound of car tyres and wet asphalt. Strips of light climb in through the window, crawl across the wall and over the ceiling. I know this room. The breathing is me. I'm still here. Everything's still here. My childhood bedroom: birdcage, piles of books, the radiator… I close my wide-open eyes, they spring right back open again. I turn this way and that, lay my hands on my body to soothe it, to bring on sleep, to make it believe there's someone there. There is an unfamiliar smell on the pillows but that must be me too. I'm alone, I know it's good, being alone is good, it's what I want, I've decided. I eventually get up, go into the living room without turning on the light, lie on the sofa, pull the blanket up to my shoulders and watch cartoons until I fall asleep without knowing it.

It's dark and completely silent.

The carousel rattles quietly. Light flutters behind my eyes.

Birds shriek from the palm trees. I walk around my father's house. The door's open. A note on the kitchen table: *Gone to the red city, please feed the dogs.*

The suitcase lies open under the table, its edges chewed.

The dogs have eaten the kid!

I walk around the small island, through the white sand and into the jungle: green green green, beams of light and glittering diamond water droplets; there are monkeys and snakes and butterflies. And there are the dogs! They erupt out of the underbrush, and the kid is riding on the back of the smallest one, it's holding on tightly to its ears. Woohoo!

I shout: I missed you so much! Look how old I've become!

We go back to the house together and roast bananas over the fire.

The carousel has stopped. I climb out of the coffin, I leave the little house.

Crows in the trees. And nuts roll in the gravel. And a bird flies up in a clamour.

And in the little houses the dead carry on sleeping.

In the morning the sun rises and vainly looks at its reflection in the glass church. The sea has become calm.

Only a finger's breadth of colourless water laps at the bottom steps of the staircase, it's as if a meek creature is retreating to the horizon.

The soothsayer is still snoring in the tower, I can hear her from down here. I sit on the stairs and watch the suitcase being washed up: carried in and carried back off by the waves, until it lies at the foot of the staircase. I tiptoe down the stairs, my heart thumping. I click open the rusted clasps. The suitcase is empty. I sit on the stairs and cry.

Through the haze of tears I see something moving far out in the mire. I stand up and stamp down with the suitcase, now so very light. A seagull is sitting there. It has small black eyes and a broken wing. I lift it up and place it in the suitcase. I crouch down beside it. We blink.

A great shadow rises up to the sea's surface and moves towards us. The water ripples like a hundred thousand pock marks, and then it heaves itself out of the water, shining and black, mightily snorting and gurgling. We wade out to him, the whale opens its mouth, and I carefully steady the suitcase and climb into the darkness.

In the abdominal cavity is a barrel with a small candle and a typewriter on it. I put down the suitcase bearing the injured seagull beneath a gland leaking healing water and sit at the barrel. The whale snorts out of its blowhole, the walls of its stomach expand and draw back together.

You're right, I say, I'm like you. I have the same illness: wanting everything. To know everything, to feel everything, to experience everything! As much of the world as can fit into a life, that's what I want. And even more. And then I feel like a thief.

What is happiness? Staying put, yes, happiness is without suspense. Clinging to happiness is cowardly. There's nothing great about it. Happiness is for small minded people. The last thing I need is to make a child for Seifert because he wants one. Then I can go to parties with Mabel and kiss other people, while Seifert stays home making porridge. That's how it's going to be. I know how it went for you, and I still stay in the little house and blame everyone else because nothing's going on. But where should I go? If I leave I'll never find anyone who loves me as much as Seifert does.

It's horrible. We stick with the first person we don't find unbearable just so we're not alone. And to prove to ourselves that we can do it we go the whole hog, brick ourselves in with promises and obligations and close off all the ways that could lead to something new and exciting.

Where would we be then!

I'm like a flounder in a fish market. I know that I'm in the wrong place; my life, my sea is only a few metres away, but I have neither the energy nor the legs to make it back. It's much more pleasant to just stay lying there, breathing shallowly, and waiting for salvation.

Yes, I could do it just like you did, I could stay and wait until I explode or pine away. Or I can do it differently and be more how I want to be.

Do you know what thought I had recently? I thought, when I'm grown up – and then I realised: I am grown up. It's now. I can brush my teeth whenever I want, and when I don't want to I don't. I can join a communist football club, bellow songs in the village square, finally feel like I belong. Or not. But now I can and must do what I always wanted to do, what I want to do now. Otherwise it won't ever happen.

I can't hear if he's still responding. I quickly run a sheet of paper in the typewriter and tap on the keys until there's a droning in my ears, my fingers are numb, my nails are broken, and I keep going and don't stop.

A gust of wind whirls the pages from the barrel, light floods the stomach room, and the seagull sluggishly puffs itself up. I look up and see the sky. The whale has opened its mouth. I climb up its throat, we're back at the castle. The seagull sits on the whale's nose, they've become friends.

The sun is rising. Mabel's head is lying on my leg, her hands are over her face balled into fists, a pool of slobber is spreading across my trousers.

The early morning light really is the most beautiful, it makes people radiant. Even Mabel's moustache has a golden shimmer, and in the saliva on my trousers bacteria sparkle, and everything is softened by a rosy-yellow morning filter.

I gently lay Mabel's head on the floor and stand up.

Seifert is lying nestled on the stairs, his head is hanging down over the edge of a step. I feel in his pocket and fish out a cigarette paper that has a line for a new song written on it. *There are no solutions, and we never arrive.* I screw it up and keep looking for the key.

I march up to the car, kick away a beer can, open the door, climb in. Underneath the clutch is Seifert's bag, I take out a cereal bar and drop the bag out of the window. Then I turn the key in the ignition, put it in gear and drive back out the driveway, crunching the gravel under the tyres. When I get onto the coastal road I turn the radio on. The sea blinks below me. The sun shines straight in my face.

Acknowledgements

For their inspiration and quotes I'd like to thank the miracle worker Daniil Kharms, along with Schlager-Reinheart and the pirates from The Decemberists.

And everyone who came along for the ride.

Thanks

Thank you to Jen and Theodora.

Thank you to the Istituto Svizzero Rome and Pro Helvetia.